A Rainy Night
and
Other Short Stories

Fred Hinkley

Fredrick Hudgin

Novels
The End of Children Series:
    The Beginning of the End
    The Three-Hour War
    The Emissary
Ghost Ride
School of the Gods
Green Grass
Sulphur Springs
A Rainy Night and other Short Stories
    (My Short Story Collection)

Poetry Collection
Four Winds

Fredrick Hudgin

A Rainy Night
and
Other Short Stories

This is a work of fiction. Names, characters, places, and incidents either are the product of the author's imagination or are used fictitiously, and any resemblance to actual persons, living or dead, business establishments, events, or locales is entirely coincidental.

A Rainy Night and Other Short Stories

Copyright 2024 by Fredrick Hudgin

All rights reserved
No part of this book may be reproduced, scanned, or distributed in any printed or electronic form without permission. Please do not participate in or encourage piracy of copyrighted materials in violation of the author's rights. Purchase only authorized editions.

ISBN: 978-1544673899

Printed in the United States of America

I wrote my first short story while taking Creative Writing at Purdue University in 1967. It was the only course I passed. A cute graduate student taught the class. She encouraged me and criticized my work until both of us were satisfied. After the semester ended, we both went our separate ways—me to Vietnam, her to the next class of freshmen. I would like to meet again so I could say thanks.

This collection is dedicated to her.

A teacher touches many lives
and hardly ever knows who is affected or how.

Fredrick Hudgin

"Short stories are tiny windows into other worlds and other minds and other dreams. They are journeys you can make to the far side of the universe and still be back in time for dinner."
— Neil Gaiman

Table of Contents

A Rainy Night 1
The Captain's Gold 7
Ashes on the Ocean 16
The Job 20
Being Dad 24
Get Them OFF! 32
Gina 36
Paradise 54
The Longest Ride 62
It's Up to Jack 69
A Call in the Middle of the Night 76
Nice Day for a Ride 80
Ha 88
Who Was Eve Really? 91
The Chair 108
Coming Home 109
The Beer Drinkers Guide to the Universes 123
The Mission 129
The Second Chance 134
The Wiz 141
They Don't Have Christmas in Vietnam 147
When Is a Kiss Not a Kiss 151
Author's Notes 154
Fredrick Hudgin 159

A Rainy Night

A black line of clouds formed as I drove my old car up the narrow road that seemed to stretch endlessly in front of me. The trees blocked most of my view, but this would be a wet night from what I could see. The sky lit up with a lightning flash, followed by another, then a third.

"Four o'clock, and it's already dark as night. Damn!"

I pulled into a wide spot on the shoulder and took off my glasses, attempting to clean the dandruff, dust, and oily dirt from them. All I accomplished was smearing it around a little. Another brilliant flash destroyed my night vision for a moment. That exit from the interstate had seemed like such a great idea. "Get off the super slab and see some of the country!"

I had been driving in and out of the Appalachians for most of the day, heading down to Huntsville to visit some friends. My friends didn't know my schedule. I had no timetable to keep. A side trip to enjoy the fall color had seemed so cool! Maybe not so much anymore.

Another bolt erupted from the clouds, closer this time—the rumble breaking through the tired woman's voice singing a tired country song on my tired AM radio.

"I hated that song when she sang it at the Grammy's," I muttered, turning the dial from one end to the other: Mexican music, advertisements, a preacher telling me that

Jesus had died for the sins I wouldn't make for another 2,000 years. The speaker rattled every time the preacher's voice hit a low note. I turned it off.

Flash – BOOM! The hair on the back of my neck stood up. "Too damned close!" I complained nervously, putting on the brakes and straining my neck to see up into the clouds: just blackness. Then, something moved at the edge of the headlight beam in front of the car. I turned so the lights could shine on it. A sign hung by one chain, blowing back and forth in the wind, giving an eerie moan-squeak with each swing—Blue Bayou Bed and Breakfast. I could barely hear the squeak over the wind in the trees.

"Blue Bayou?" Outside the car's windows, I could see nothing but two-hundred-year-old oak and hickory trees, their branches meeting over the road—no river, no pond, not even a tiny stream.

"Yeah, right! Blue Bayou, my ass!" I chuckled. "Someone has an imagination." But even to me, my chuckle sounded hollow.

....

My life had been normal a month ago—good job as a computer programmer, happy family, pretty wife, two kids. Then the company I worked for had folded—no warning—just a lock on the door, and the paychecks stopped. Another employee said a Chinese conglomerate had bought the company, and our jobs were being outsourced to India. Then, two weeks later, a drunk driver killed Jamie and the kids when she was bringing them home from soccer practice. The drunk had died, too. He had two other DUIs pending in court. The funeral had been a week ago.

Jamie didn't have living parents, sisters, or brothers. Neither did I. A couple of friends from work and kids and parents from my kids' soccer teams attended the burial service. Ten minutes after the preacher finished, I stood alone, watching three fresh graves being filled by the cemetery gravediggers, working stoically in the rain with their backhoe.

"You have to leave the past behind," the shrink told me on my first and only visit—a past I still couldn't think about without a spear of pain ripping through my heart. But who could argue with logic like that? So I went home, lit a fire, and left.

....

I turned the car up the driveway, weaving around the potholes and rocks. Another flash-boom exploded nearby, taking my breath away and blinding me for a moment. Some fat raindrops began to hit the smeared bugs on the windshield. Ahead, I saw a light that slowly morphed into a house with a wrap-around porch, the paint faded and peeling. A sign swung back and forth over the door in the middle of the porch, saying "Welcome."

I parked the car beside an ancient oak tree, briefly illuminated by a lightning flash, its branches clawing into the darkness above me. The downpour started in earnest as I closed the car door, beating down in sheets. There might as well have been a fire hose directly over me. I got soaked as I ran to the front door and dove through the waterfall coming off the roof. The door opened before I could knock, the roar of the rain smothering any noise the door made. A little girl with huge dark eyes, maybe ten, stared back at me from behind the screen door as I shivered in the dark.

"You need a room. Come in." She pushed open the door and beckoned me to enter.

The entrance hall appeared as run-down as the paint on the outside of the house. A fake Tiffany lamp on a worn end table near the door gave a faint illumination to the hallway. The walls were covered with yellowed photographs of people who stared out at me like wraiths from a different universe. A staircase ascended one side of the hallway, disappearing into the upstairs dark.

"Mother will be down in a moment," the little girl said as she closed the door. The sound of the deluge outside lowered to a dull roar. "We don't get many visitors here since they finished the interstate. You can wait in there."

She pointed through a doorway into the living room. I sat in one of the threadbare chairs and studied the room while waiting. A worn, twisted-rag rug filled the middle of the floor. Over the unlit fireplace were pictures of men in uniform who looked like they should still be in high school. The mantle had a folded American flag in a triangular walnut case with a small brass plaque on the glass in front. Beside the fireplace, an open doorway lead outside with only a screen door to keep the wind and rain out. The noise of the storm filled the room through the opening. The wind bumped the door every so often, giving off a soft *thump* as the door struggled against the latch. I got up to swing the door shut.

"Don't close it," the girl said quietly.

I jumped. She was right beside me, and I hadn't heard her approach. The downpour outside must have covered her footsteps. "You like to hear the storm?" I asked, walking over to the fireplace. Maybe I could start a fire.

"Not particularly. Mother likes it open. She's sure dad's coming home."

"Where's he been?" I rubbed my wet arms, willing them warm—my wet short-sleeved white shirt clung to my arms and torso like a second skin.

"Afghanistan." Those sad, dark eyes filled her face. "He left home a year ago today."

"Well, he should be coming back soon."

"He'll never be coming back. He got blown to bits with two of his friends. There wasn't enough left to bury."

I tried to hide my shock at her nonchalance. "When did it happen?"

"One hundred ninety-three days ago."

I glanced at the open door and began to understand. Mom was having a little trouble dealing with it. I had some empathy with that, a lot actually.

"Is that who the flag is for?" I indicated the flag on the mantle.

"No. They gave us that for Uncle Kevin. He got it in Iraq five years ago."

I didn't know what to say. She'd lost both her dad and her uncle in her short life.

"Mom's convinced Dad and his two friends will come walking through that door tonight in their desert camouflage uniforms, looking like they did when they left a year ago."

I kept looking between the flag and the open door with no idea what to say.

She stared sadly out into the rain. "Dad's dog, Jessie, ran off after he died. I miss him, even if he was a little screwy. I think he got stuck in quicksand down by the river."

"Why was he screwy?"

"He hated strangers, *especially* men—made it hard to run a bed-and-breakfast with him trying to bite anything in pants. The last guy he bit needed twenty stitches; some were a little personal."

I stood up as a pretty, middle-aged woman walked into the room.

"Hi. I'm Teresa." She waved her hand at the door. "I apologize for the open door, but I'm expecting my husband and friends to return at any moment."

I looked at her with infinite sadness. She really didn't have a clue they were dead.

On the porch, I heard footsteps. Three armed men in desert camouflage walked in as the screen door swung open, followed by a muscular Rottweiler that put its ears down and started growling at me.

"Hi, Honey!" Teresa said, smiling. "Right on time."

I gave a panicked look at her, the men, and the dog, then screamed and ran out the front door into the rain. I jumped into my car and spun mud all over the courtyard as I raced down the driveway and onto the road.

Teresa stared at where the taillights had disappeared with her mouth still open. Finally, she turned to her daughter with a raised eyebrow. "Now, what was *that* all about?"

"It's probably Jessie," her daughter announced, a serious expression on her face. "That guy had just gotten back from Afghanistan. He said the Taliban had ambushed his patrol, and he had survived by hiding in a small cave nearby. The Taliban had surrounded the cave and sicced their dogs on him to pull him out. He fought them off with his razor-sharp bayonet while they bit at his legs. The Taliban fighters just laughed and laughed while their dogs tore at him. They didn't hear the rest of his patrol sneaking up behind them until they felt the patrol's bullets tearing them apart. The patrol killed them all *and* the dogs. He had one of the animal's ears on a chain around his neck."

All five of the adults were silent, staring at her incredulously. She smiled back, satisfied.

Finally, her father chuckled and rolled his eyes. "We got a deer, hon." He kissed his wife on the cheek. "We'll be out in the barn dressin' it."

"OK, Pete. Dinner's ready when you are."

Pete turned to his daughter. "And *you*, young lady! Go down to the road and take down that sign that keeps *magically* reappearing every time it rains. Do it now, before another poor soul comes up here looking for shelter, and you scare him to death, too. This place hasn't been a bed-and-breakfast since Kevin sold it to us and moved to Tallahassee five years ago."

The Captain's Gold

He was a sailor on that beautiful boat. It left a trail of white foam and swung into the wind, sails billowing. My little town wrapped around the bay where they anchored. Someone had carved a naked woman into the front of the boat underneath the bowsprit. She didn't look happy ... I should have heeded her warning.

I laughed at the crew as they filed off the ship onto the quay, eager to spend their wages in the bars and brothels of our town. Boats landed here all the time. The merchants of our town tolerated the sailors' excesses for as long as their money lasted. However, the captains they treated with homage and respect. He bought their goods and carried them to other ports, just as he sold them goods from around the world. Without the captains, the merchants would founder. Without the sailors, there would be no captains.

To me, a barmaid, they were all entertainment. I served them brandy, beer, wine, and occasionally food. They tipped me well and patted my behind, hoping for a kiss or more. I'd flirt and watch that fill their egos, but all they'd ever get from me was a wish and a smile. In a day or three, the tide would wash them back into the ocean, and my town would wait for the next ship of fools to arrive.

On the crew's first night ashore, I usually worked late. Sometimes one of those love-starved sailors got a little overzealous in his amorous pursuits, but my departure routine had never failed. At the end of my shift, I left the Inn of the Dragon in stealth. A man's coat and hat covered my dress and long hair. I took all of the back ways to avoid any confrontation. I had just turned the last corner to my home, looking forward to putting my feet up and enjoying a warm cup of tea, when I felt a hand grip my arm like a steel band.

"It's too early to go home, my pretty," he whispered.

I recognized him, the captain of the ship. He'd been at the inn and bought his crew drinks all night. I tried to pull my arm away, but he wouldn't release me. He pulled me close and grabbed my breast. "How about a kiss? I think I've paid for it."

"Release her!" a voice behind him commanded.

"And if I don't?" The captain didn't even turn around.

"I'll gut you like a cod and feed your entrails to the dogs. It's better than you deserve."

His eyes went hard. He dropped my arm and pulled his sword free of the scabbard.

The two of them circled, trading slashes and thrusts, their swords ringing when they hit. I hesitated, clutching the knife I carried. Would the captain resume his pursuit of me after the fight? Should I run while I can? Should I leave the man who rescued me from a rapist? What if he gets hurt? What if he gets killed? No! Not if I can help it!

A cut appeared on the captain's cheek. A feint, a parry, a thrust, and the captain's sword impaled the side of his attacker's abdomen. A moment later, I'd made my decision. He leaned over to retrieve his sword. Then his expression changed from victory to disbelief as he felt the blade of my knife slide across his throat. Blood erupted under his chin. Instead of assaulting me, he clutched his throat, attempting to staunch the flow, then sank to his knees and died, his eyes empty and soulless.

The wounded man who had come to my defense lay on the ground, the captain's sword still through his side.

"Pull it out!" he hissed.

I grabbed the hilt and pulled, trying to follow the penetration line. He gasped but didn't move. Blood flowed out both the entry and exit wounds. "Pull off my coat and shirt. Use the shirt as a bandage."

He gasped as I pulled the shirt tight. The makeshift bandage helped a little. Blood still seeped out both sides, but not nearly as fast. I put his jacket around his shoulders.

"Get the captain's purse. It's on his belt."

"I'm no thief!"

"If we take the money, everyone will think a robber did this. Or would you like to be a murderer? I think there's still some room left on those gallows by the harbor."

The city magistrate left people hanging on the gallows as a warning to sailors when they landed. And it worked. Most sailors were on their best behavior in our town as they sampled the plethora of vices made available to them. I cut loose the purse.

"Now, I need a place to stay for a few days until I can ride a horse."

My subconscious was going overtime. *Do you think no one heard them fighting? That no one is going to look for the captain's assailant? What are you doing, Geri? This guy is nothing to you. You mean nothing to him.*

I fought back. *This one is different. He saved me from being raped. No one has saved me from anything since my parents died.*

After draping his coat over his shoulders, I put his arm over my shoulder, and together we walked the short distance to my tiny house on the edge of town. We passed no one. No faces appeared in the windows. He collapsed into my bed and passed out with a sigh. I undressed him and washed the blood from his body. *What is he like?* I wondered. *Why did he save me from the captain? Was he a pirate? Where did he come from? Would he leave when he healed? Did he have a lover? Did he have a wife?* I felt my heart flip-flop at the thought of him with another woman. *Stop that!* I scolded myself. *He'll leave me as soon as he can. Until then, I will protect him as he protected me.*

I studied the injury. It wasn't as bad as I'd thought—through the muscle, but not any organs. It would make quite a scar. There were other scars on his body. Each one probably had a story about its making. I made an actual bandage and applied it along with some salve I'd gotten from the barber for nicked fingers. The blood flow had almost stopped. I pulled the covers up to his neck and sat in the chair next to the bed staring at his face. I didn't even know his name.

How long did I stare at him? I have no idea. I woke up with the dawn, stiff from sleeping in the chair. Sometime in the night, I must have wrapped a blanket around myself. I stared at the man in panic. *Is he dead?* Then his chest rose under the covers. *He's alive!... and his eyes are open and looking at me.* I realized with a start.

"My name is Mykal," he said.

Somewhere in my throat, there were vocal cords. And they could speak. "I am Geri."

"I used the bedpan last night. You looked so cold, so I put the blanket around you."

"Thanks." *That explained the blanket. He had been run through with a sword and worried about me being cold!*

"How are you feeling?" I asked. "How are your wounds?"

"Sore. I'll live. I've had worse. I thought the captain was drunker, or I'd have been more careful."

"Why are you here? Why were you in that alley last night?"

"I saw you leave and watched the captain follow you. I am one of his crew. He was an evil man. I knew what he would do."

"What will happen to you now? Where will you go?"

"I need to buy a horse and leave town. When they find the captain and I don't show up today, the first officer will figure out what happened. The captain and I weren't exactly friends."

Someone pounded on the door. I pulled a shawl around my shoulders and opened it.

The town constable stood there. "Geri, are you alright?"

"Sure, Enoge. Why wouldn't I be?"

"The ship's captain got murdered last night, not far from here. Did you hear anything?"

"I didn't hear a sound."

The constable saw Mykal reclining in my bed, and his face turned as red as his wine-infused nose. "Well, then." He cleared his throat. "See you later."

"We have to burn the bloody clothes and leave!" I hissed after the door closed.

"Why?"

"This is a small town. Someone saw us. You two weren't exactly being quiet. Enoge will find a witness, and then he will come back for us. We will hang side by side on that gallows. This town protects its captains."

I grabbed our clothes from last night and fanned the coals in the fireplace into a roaring fire. Then, one by one, I fed the clothes into the flames.

"Wait!" he called as I tossed his shirt in.

"What?" I asked, looking at the door.

"You just burned my only clothes."

I pulled out the basket of laundry on the floor the innkeeper had given me to wash yesterday. "See if any of these fit you."

I washed the blood off Mykal's boots, his sword, and my knife then rolled up a bundle of clothes in a blanket for the trip. *Trip to where? Are you going with him? What are you doing, Geri? This is the only place you've ever been. You don't even know if he wants you along.*

While he looked for clothes, I emptied the captain's purse, threw the leather bag in the fire, and sewed the gold coins into a fold inside my bodice. We left the house and walked to the stable. The stable owner, Stive, had taught me how to ride and always flirted with me.

"Geri!" he greeted me, giving me a hug and a kiss on my cheek. "How are you this fine day?"

"I'm wonderful, Stive. I want to go riding with my friend. Have you got two good horses we can buy?"

He eyed Mikal curiously but didn't question me about him. I didn't usually ride with company. "For you, I have the perfect horse. Gentle and obedient. Unless you'd like a wild stallion?" He wiggled his eyebrows in a lewd grin.

"Gentle sounds perfect." I stretched up and kissed his cheek. "What do you have for Mykal?"

"I'd like that bay gelding," Mykal said, eyeing the horse with appreciation.

"You have an eye for horses, sir. I'll get them saddled."

I gave him a gold coin.

"Geri, are you leaving? Forever?"

"Tips have been good at the Inn. Good-bye, Stive." I hugged him again.

I tied my small blanket bundle behind my saddle. We swung onto the horses and trotted out of town. As soon as we passed the last houses, Mykal changed into a gallop, and we ran the horses until they were winded. A spot of blood appeared on his shirt. He seemed to be favoring his side, so we walked for a while until the horses got their breath back, then started the smooth, slow canter a healthy horse can do all day long.

While we rode, I had time to reconsider what I had done and where this was going. I had no one left since my parents had died aboard a ship that foundered in a storm years ago. Many men wanted to share my bed, but none wanted a lover. I had no future in that town. Lately, my dreams had been filled with a child's voice asking me to birth them. I was sure it was a little girl. Was Mykal the one? I tried to see into the future, but, as usual, it remained just out of sight.

We camped next to a small creek a mile off the road that night. Since we arrived at our campsite, it was like fire passed between us every time we touched. I studied my hand the first time it happened, looking for a reason, maybe a splinter. The shock of that touch went to the core of where I kept my "woman." Then, I felt those hidden muscles clench again. And each time after that, it got worse, or better, depending on how you thought about it. I'd never had feelings like this before. I didn't know what to do with them. Mykal must have been feeling it, too. Our attempts at conversation were awkward.

Finally, I'd had enough. I had to find out, so I kissed him. It was like no other kiss in my life. His tongue probed my mouth and mine, his. He tasted sweet and clean. That kiss began at my mouth and went straight to *there*. I felt myself moisten. This was where I was meant to be—in his arms, being kissed like this. I'd never believed it was possible to have these feelings—so desired, so desirable. I felt his hands move across my back and longed for them to go lower. *Grab me! Grasp me! Take me! Right here! Right now! Would he? Could he?*

I heard my unconceived daughter's voice call to me. *Please, mom!* Time to throw caution to the wind. For better or worse, this is going to happen. I began to undo my bodice and stepped out of my skirt. He opened his pants and took off his shirt. The blood on his bandage made me hesitate. Then he pulled me into his arms.

We lay on our clothes. He was beside me. He ran his hands down my body, leaving trails of fire behind them on my skin. He took one nipple in his mouth and rolled it. The nerve endings were connected straight to those hidden muscles. They clenched again. I arched my back and moaned. I was so ready for him. He took my other nipple, played with it, and then trailed his mouth lower, leaving a path of liquid fire behind. He reached my navel and paused while he gripped the area gently with his teeth and drilled into me with his tongue. Then he continued his path lower, down to my center. Waves of pleasure coursed through me. He put one finger into me, then two while he licked and sucked on my little button. I gasped, arched, and dissolved into a million pieces.

He shifted and began kissing me again, on my lips this time. I tasted me on his lips. I felt his member enter me, fill me. In one thrust, he was buried inside, stretching my secret place. I wrapped my legs around him, hugged him to my chest, and then felt something melt in my heart. He began to move. Nothing in this life had prepared me for how good he felt, how much I wanted him right *there*. He picked up his pace. His breath was coming in ragged gasps. I felt the pressure building inside me again. Without any thought, I grabbed him with all my might and dissolved a second time. I'd never experienced an orgasm before that night. Now I was having my second in five minutes! It washed over me again and again as Mykal moved in rhythm with me. I didn't know if it would ever end, didn't want it to, hoped it wouldn't. I felt him fill me with his orgasm as he went rigid. Slowly, the world returned to focus, but it would never be "normal" again—not with Mykal in my life. The only thing I wanted to do was do it again—with him, all day, all night, forever.

We fell asleep, still in each other's arms.

"Seize them!" a voice said.

The soldiers grabbed the two of us. We were trussed, blindfolded, and put on our horses. At least the magistrate allowed us to put on our clothes before we were tied.

As we re-entered the village, I'd never heard it so quiet. I sat in the jail, separate from Mykal, for a week. Finally, the magistrate summoned me to his chambers. We were alone when I entered.

"You have a choice," he told me. "You can become my willing mistress, and your friend will be allowed to escape, or I will sentence you both to be executed."

I thought about the choices. *Die with Mykal or die without him.*

"What guarantee can you make for his safe passage?"

"I will have him join the crew of the next boat. That's the best I can do. Whether he lives or dies after that is up to him."

"Can I talk to him about it?"

"No."

"When I see him leave on the boat, I will agree."

Ten days later, I watched my love leave with the tide. I smiled, realizing that my one day with Mykal would last me for the rest of my life. That night as the magistrate pounded into me, I closed my eyes and imagined Mykal and me together on that boat as we sailed into the setting sun. Nine months later, I had a baby girl with curly blonde hair and hazel eyes. I loved her as no other child had ever been loved. I named her Myka.

We rode Mykal's bay gelding every day; Myka strapped in front of my chest in a sling. Some days we rode into the mountains. Some days we rode along the coast. Myka loved those rides as much as I did. One day we passed a deserted beach. I tied the gelding where he could get fresh water from a stream and some grass nearby, then carried Myka as we strolled beside the breakers coming in from the ocean. The sun-warmed beach caressed my feet. Mykal had left a year ago. Ahead of us, I saw something white, partially covered in the sand. I dug around it with a piece of driftwood. A human skeleton slowly appeared with some curly blonde hair still attached. Mykal's clothes, the clothes he took from the basket in my house, the clothes he wore when he left on the boat, were still on him. His skull had a hole in it. They had killed him and thrown him overboard as soon as they left the harbor.

I walked back to the gelding and mounted. We turned away from the village toward the mountains and a new life, the captain's gold heavy in my bodice.

Ashes on the Ocean

The front door closing echoed through our little house like a funeral drum. Nothing greeted me but a dust ball, slowly tumbling across the floor from the puff of tepid air I'd let in. I put my frayed pocketbook on the old sofa Mother had given us as a wedding present and sat down heavily, alone at last.

He had died—Thomas, my husband of forty-three years—dead and gone; nothing left of him but this little urn of ashes, cradled in my lap; nothing but this urn and forty-four years of memories.

I looked around the room, feeling like I'd never been there before: worn-out furniture, a threadbare carpet, and nicotine stains on the walls from forty-three years of Thomas sitting in his armchair, smoking one cigarette after another, while he gazed mindlessly at the television.

There were no pictures of children on the fireplace mantle—we had no children of our own; not since that day in November so many years ago: November 16th—the day of the end of children. He wouldn't let me name her. He wouldn't even let me bury the tiny body of my first-born, my only-born daughter. The nurse put her tiny corpse on the gurney, dead before it lived. I never saw my daughter again.

"Alice," I said to the empty house, "her name was Alice. Why didn't you let me hold her at least once?" But he wouldn't, and then the nurse did what she does with dead babies.

Every year after that, on November 16th, when he'd gone to work on workdays or to McDoughal's on weekends, I'd get out the cupcake I'd smuggled home. I'd stick a single candle into the icing, sing Happy Birthday to Alice, blow out the candle, and eat the cupcake, pretending I'd tasted the chocolate for the first time. Then I would open all the imaginary presents I bought for Alice, one by one. Together we laughed, sang, and played with the toys.

The ceremony slowly changed as Alice grew older. Imaginary teddy bears gave way to imaginary bicycles, which changed into imaginary phonograph records. Our fun continued until Thomas's footsteps echoed on the front porch.

One year Thomas found the cupcake and must have thought I'd bought it for him. I found the paper sleeve in the trash on top of yesterday's newspaper. That was the only year Alice had an imaginary cupcake to go with the imaginary toys. Alice hadn't seemed to notice.

Thomas quit sleeping in our bed after Alice's birth-death. He said he didn't want children. He never *asked*—he just *said*. That was Thomas. Dinner on the table when he got home: meatloaf on Monday, pasta on Tuesday, steak on Wednesday, casserole on Thursday, fish on Friday, chicken on Saturday, and ham on Sunday—every week, every month, every year—for forty-three years.

And now he's gone. Today is Tuesday. I got up from the sofa and walked into the kitchen, pulling out two of the construction trash bags Thomas kept on the back porch. I filled them with all the groceries on the shelves in the pantry and fridge, dividing them into perishables and non-perishables. The perishables I put into the trashcan beside the house. The non-perishables went into the trunk of Thomas's old Dodge. No need for this stuff to go to waste— St. Augustine's had a food drive going on right now— someone would want it.

I packed all of Thomas's clothes and bathroom stuff into more trash bags and put them next to the groceries in the trunk. Goodwill would find a new home for the stuff that wasn't worn out.

On the way home, I stopped at the grocery store and filled a cart with all of the food Thomas never let me buy: fresh vegetables, fresh fruit, half-and-half, couscous, coconut milk, hot sauce, almonds, caffeinated coffee, and vanilla bean ice cream.

It felt so delicious to break the rules, rules I'd lived with for forty-three years. I bought a real birthday cake from the bakery section: a pink buttercream icing carrot cake with "Happy Birthday Alice" on top in chocolate with enough birthday candles to put twenty-eight on top.

At the hardware store, I bought five gallons of paint. Not the pale blue that Thomas had used forty-three years ago when he'd painted the inside of our house for the first and only time. Instead, I bought bright, happy colors the clerk said would go together.

When I got home, I found a stray dog pawing at the garbage can. It looked barely grown and about half-starved to death. I pulled out a package of hamburger from the stuff I'd thrown away and cooked it for the dog. It cringed away from me as I put the overflowing bowl on the ground, then quickly returned to scarf down the meat. As the dog finished, it looked up at me hopefully. Shaking my head and laughing simultaneously, I rooted around in the food I'd discarded and found a steak and some spaghetti. I cooked it, then watched the dog gobble my offering. After he finished the food, he plopped down on the back porch like he belonged there and went to sleep.

I chuckled at what Thomas would have said: "What're you thinkin', woman! I ain't feedin' no goddammed dog!"

I pulled the blanket and pillow off Thomas's bed and spread it out for the dog, gagging on the cigarette smell. The dog would have to decide if it stayed or left.

I cleaned, painted, and reorganized the house for the rest of the week. Some of the furniture I just put out on the curb. Thomas's armchair and the living room carpet were beyond help. The smell of cigarettes would never leave them. His bed—same story. I tied the mattress and springs on top of the Dodge and made a trip to the landfill. I finally had a sewing room where his bed had been. I put Mother's sewing machine on his desk.

I named the dog Bill. He'd decided to stay, so the blanket and pillow got a wash, and so did Bill. His first bath was an experience for both of us, but the fleas had to go, and down the drain they went. I'd never had a dog, and apparently, Bill had never had a human. Slowly we worked out how to live together.

Sunday, I gave Alice her first real birthday party. We laughed and took turns holding Meredith, Alice's new baby girl. Alice loved Bill. He curled up at her feet and got his piece of cake with a big scoop of ice cream.

After the party, I decided my life-after-Thomas was well underway. The time had come. He always said he wanted to have his ashes spread at sea. The nearest ocean was five hundred miles away. It would take a while to get there—but a promise is a promise.

I picked up the urn from the mantle over the fireplace, walked into the bathroom, carefully poured his ashes into the toilet, and then pressed the flush lever. The ashes swirled around and around as they dissolved into the water. Thomas had told me many times all water ends up in the ocean. It took three flushes before the last of Thomas began its underground journey to the sea.

I stared at the toilet for a few moments as the sound of water running into the tank behind it filled the room. Thomas had spent forty-three years telling me my job was to support him in whatever he decided to do—support him without resistance or criticism.

"I wonder how far he'll get today," I asked the empty room thoughtfully, then smiled as I took a seat. "I might as well help him along on his trip. I mean, what else are wives for?"

The Job

"Miles, we need to talk."

His mother had the impossibly annoying habit of interrupting him every time he began to win at WOW (World of Warcraft). Cymry Nettled had been vanquished. Hestuunrune was hiding. And he had killed his arch-enemy, Quberus, for the time being.

"Give me a minute, Mom," he said in exasperation. "I'll take out the garbage as soon as I'm done."

"Nope, not this time." She pushed the button on the power strip. His quest disappeared into a black screen.

"Great!" he shook his head, making his greasy hair swing in front of his eyes. "Now Hestuunrune will take over the world. Thanks!"

"It's a *game*, Miles."

He ignored her blasphemy. "What do you want, Mom?"

"Miles, you are twenty-seven. You've been a freshman at Portland State for seven years. You've never had a job that lasted more than one month, even during the two years you took off after high school. It's time."

"Time for what? How can I keep a job when I'm going to college to get a degree that I can support myself with? I just can't find a major that works for me."

She handed him the letter she had received today. "They kicked you out, Miles." She held up her hand and ticked off all of his attempted majors. "First you chose African Studies, then Comics Studies, then Film studies, then

Jazz Studies, then Woman Studies, then ... what was the last one?"

"Revitalizing Endangered Indigenous Languages."

"Yeah. How did that go?"

"I got lost in Navaho."

"Navaho? Really?"

"They used it in World War II to talk in the Pacific theater. The Japanese couldn't figure it out."

"Neither could you. College is done. It's time for you to get a job."

"What do you want me to do, Mom? Mow the lawn? Weed the flowerbeds? Pick up my room?"

"No, a job—you know—a place you go every day, a place where you do something for someone, and they pay you for it."

"So, you want me to work at McDonald's?"

"McDonald's has a career path. They will pay for any job-related college courses."

"Job-related courses for McDonald's. Let me see, what would they be? —Accounting, business administration, marketing, economics? I suck at math."

"And English, geography, history, even basket weaving."

"I *never* took *basket weaving*! Only *pussies* take basket weaving."

She handed him a card. "Here's the card from a guy at the State Employment Agency. He said he could help you find something." Miles held the card using the tips of two fingers like it was radioactive, and he might overdose from too much skin contact. "His name is Gordon Tradenik, pronounced tra-den-ik. We talked today after I got that letter. He's expecting you there tomorrow at 8 A.M. He said he's had a lot of experience helping kids enter the workplace and is looking forward to meeting you."

"8 A.M.? Why so late? Couldn't you have made it six or even *five*? How about midnight? Now that's an appointment

I could have enjoyed. We could meet at Ground Control Arcade, have a beer, check out the girls...."

"8 A.M. at the Employment Office. Which means you need to leave here at 7:30 to catch the bus, which means you get up at 6:30."

"It's not even daylight at 6:30."

"And you know that how?"

He smiled at her proudly. "I'm usually just coming in about then."

She tried not to laugh. "You be at Gordon's desk tomorrow at 8 A.M., or everything you own will be on the sidewalk tomorrow afternoon with a sign that says 'Free', including this $3,000 gaming computer your dad bought you last Christmas."

"That's MINE. You can't do that!"

"Bet me! And I'll change the locks on the doors." She gave him a cold stare. "Don't show up at Gordon's desk tomorrow and find out if I'm bluffing."

"OK." He reached for the power button, knocking over the Dead Guy ale he had balanced on his rotund belly. "*Great!*" This day just kept getting better.

She put her hand on top of his and looked directly into his eyes. "I'm not kidding."

"*OK.* I'll be there."

....

"Hi, Miles. Thanks for being on time and filling out your background forms."

"I didn't have much choice."

"Your mother seems to be very interested in your future."

"My mother thinks that because I live at home, she can control my life."

Gordon studied the forms that Miles had filled out. After a few minutes, he put the forms in a neat stack in front of him. "OK. You haven't been too successful in your past employments. Maybe you didn't find the right job. Let's start there—what *would* your ultimate dream job be?"

"What would I want to do?" Miles got a soft smile on his face and looked out the window. "I want to work in an office with lots of bright young people who love to do computer gaming. I want a healthy six figures for a salary. I want medical insurance with no co-pays and no limits. I want a cute secretary. I want a 401K plan with 100% matching contributions. I want to work within walking distance from home or have a chauffeur pick me up in a limo. I want two months of vacation a year with lots of company-paid travel all over the world." Miles paused, then added. "And no drug screenings." He smiled again. "Yeah, that should do it."

Gordon cocked his head a little, deep in thought. He pulled his keyboard to him and started typing. He spent five minutes examining his screen, retyping, and re-examining. Finally, he sighed. "The only job I can find that's even close to what you want is a guy in Europe looking for a stable companion for his super-model daughter. She's only seventeen, but according to him, she's kind of a nymphomaniac. She travels worldwide doing photoshoots, and her father needs a companion to accompany her and keep her out of trouble. He would have to be beside her wherever they went, and she always travels in first class. The job has a $200K salary, reimbursement for all expenses, a substantial clothing allowance, and three months of vacation a year while they relax at their villa on the French Riviera, where he can join them if he likes. Oh, and it has a full medical/dental/eye plan with no co-pays and no limits. The only negative is that he would have to share an apartment with his daughter at all the gigs, so he can keep tabs on her nighttime activities and visitors. Interested?"

"That's unbelievable. Are you kidding?"

"Of course I am, but you started it."

Being Dad

It's raining. I usually love the sound and smell of the rain. I love how it takes the dust and garbage we leave behind and washes it away, leaving a freshly scrubbed world for me to ride my aging motorcycle through. But not today. Today it sounds like the Gods are weeping.

Those rain sounds on the windows of this cheap motel room echo through the empty halls of my mind. Just one thought rattles around with them, eclipsing all those *urgent* things that had filled it yesterday. Yesterday—was it only yesterday when the world was normal? Last night I got a phone call from my ex, the first one in years. "Bill is dead," she said. "An IED got him while his squad was on patrol. His body will be home on Monday." Seventeen words that ended my life as I knew it.

The only thing that remains out of the ashes of yesterday's life is to ride home to bury my son—nothing else even exists. He died on a dusty street in a little village no one had ever heard of, trying to help people who didn't want him there. Thank you, Mr. Ex-President Bush. I guess my son wasn't as important as the Weapons of Mass Destruction that didn't exist or the nuclear technology we couldn't find. I don't know what we are doing there or why so many young people had to die. Guess it doesn't matter anymore. My son is dead. I'm too numb to be angry yet.

I remember your birth. I waited down near the business end of the process until you slid out into the doctor's hands. During the ultrasounds, your mom and I had deliberately not looked for your gender. So, until that moment, we had no idea if you would be a boy or a girl. It made no difference to me—I was so ready to be a dad. I looked up at your mom and announced to her, "We have a son." It took a couple of minutes for the doc to finish things with her. The nurse cleaned you, then it was all huggy-kissy, and this is what those wonderful breasts are really for. At that moment, I couldn't have loved either one of you more deeply. It justled up inside me and overflowed like a fountain of pure feel-good. If I could bottle that feeling, no drug dealer would stand a chance.

You grew up, as babies do. I made your first birthday cake from chocolate cake in the shape of a Harley. You saw the flame on top of the one candle and immediately tried to grab it. The first lesson for the day: Burning things may look pretty, but they can hurt. Somehow, eating the candle made up for your burnt finger. I could see that thought through your smile, "Bet it doesn't do that again!" It didn't take long for the cream cheese icing to make its way into your hair and nose.

You're supposed to eat it, not bathe in it, but I think you had a lot more fun rubbing it all over your face.

Kids—so many memories!

I loved giving you baths. You would splash and laugh those big belly laughs. No bath was complete until the water went up the walls and ceiling. It would be brown, and you would be clean for at least a couple of minutes. Now I have to bathe what's left of you once more, then dress you in your blues. Clean for the last time.

A circle—the world is full of circles. The wheels on my motorcycle carry me from one place in my life to another, a magical time machine taking me from the past into the future. Relationships begin, flourish, and end. Lives are born, then they die. Somehow that doesn't give me much comfort right now. His circle ended much too soon. Children are supposed to bury their parents—not the other way around.

Time to get down the road. My few things tucked into the old leather saddlebags, my rain gear on, and then roll my aging friend out of the motel room and into the rain. He fires on the first kick—no time to play games today. His lumpy idle gives me the comfort of an old friend's hug—as if he knew the pain inside me and just stood there giving what support he could.

So many places and things we have shared. You had your first ride on the back of this bike. We had you in a baby sling, secure between your mom and me—you must have been all of six months old. The ride to the club's Fourth of July party, two miles away, took about four minutes. From then on, you would cry every time I started up the bike, and you weren't going on the ride.

Onto the freeway, into the traffic. The spray from the cars covers me with water that soon finds its way into and under the rain gear. By the time it reaches those dark warm spots that really don't like to be wet or cold, I've given up even thinking about it. I guess dogs and fleas are like that—after a while, the dog quits worrying about them. They are just part of the way of life. If you ride enough, you will get wet.

We had a wet summer when I gave you your first dirt bike. I took you out to the only place within walking distance to learn to ride it—our local cemetery. By the end of the day, you were weaving in and out of those tombstones like they were gates in a slalom course. Then the skies opened up, and you learned that wet ground doesn't turn quite like dry ground. A turn, a slide, and then a crunch. Well, good! Now it's broke in. We straightened the handlebars and un-bent the shifter. Good as new. No, better! Scars are braggin' rights! Every time I heard you tell your friends about the wreck, it got bigger.

So many miles to go. It seems like this road is like a halfway house between reality and fantasy. You get the appearance of progress but are actually going nowhere. The rain is the only constant.

When you finally got your first street bike, we rode together to Lippy's. He came out to see what all that racket was. When he saw you alone on that old Honda, he stopped dead with a huge smile.

"What're you gonna name her?" he asked.

"Gayle," you responded proudly. I never did know why you chose that name, and you never told me.

Time for a pit stop. A cup of coffee sounded good. I was a hundred miles closer. Closer to what? How do you say goodbye to the only thing good you've ever done.

You always liked sugar in your coffee – from the first cup. I gave it to you like I drank it—milk, no sugar. You made a gag-me face, promptly dumped three teaspoons of sugar in it, took a big sip, and smiled.

Some things change, and some don't—that one never changed.

I'll have to remember to put some sugar in your coffin. I wouldn't want you to need it and not have any.

Back on the road—back into the gray Neverland of hopes and dreams. Cars slide slowly past me, filled with people who are oblivious to the wet, cold biker riding home—the kids in the back seat fighting over which DVD gets to be put into the player while dad listens to Green Day on his headphones and mom sleeps. Enjoy them while you can, folks. Someday they will leave.

Every lane on every road has two tire tracks worn into it, little depressed grooves about a tire width wide that countless cars and trucks have made as they passed over the road. When it rains, the grooves fill with water that motorcycles have to plow through, and cars spray all over you as they pass. As the miles roll past, the tire track I'm following begins to talk to me about the other bikes I've shared my lane with. A motorcycle can share a lane with another bike, one in each tire track, and ride two-up, but you have to trust the other rider. One small mistake, and you will both end up with a serious case of road rash. When you're lucky enough to have a rider who rides just like you do, it's like no other ride in the world. Like two birds flying in perfect formation as they weave across the sky.

You and I would ride like that for hours, knowing where each other was by instinct and trust—yet another thing I will have to bury with you in a couple of days.

A break in the clouds suddenly appears through the mist. The road is still soaking wet, but nothing could hide the rainbow that fills the sky ahead of me.

When we saw your first rainbow, I told you the story about the Leprechauns and the pot of gold. You would have nothing for it but to immediately stop the car and chase the damned thing across the countryside. We spent a great afternoon chasing that rainbow from one place to another. Then in the blink of an eye, it disappeared. I swear I heard laughing in the distance with the thunder. We went home exhausted and happy with our romp. Your mom looked at us like we were nuts when you told her about it. We got that a lot.

I guess that rainbow was signaling the end of the day, time to find another motel and get some rest. Car riders don't know how exhausting it is to ride a motorcycle in the rain. They ride along in their dial-a-temp, heated cars with cruise control, windshield wipers, CD players, and cups of coffee, passing us soggy two-wheelers without a thought. When their journey is over, they get out, stretch, and say, "What a long trip."

When we find a motel that will take bikers, we go into our rooms and spend fifteen minutes in the shower just trying to stop shivering. By then, we're so tired that even eating a meal at the greasy spoon next door is too much work, and we pass out on the bed with our clothes spread out on the chair next to the heater. Don't get me wrong—even a bad ride on a bike is better than a great ride in a car.

When you go somewhere in a car, you look out at it through the windows. The best you get is to say, "I looked out at Yosemite." When you go somewhere on a bike, you know you were there. You were part of it, and it became part of you. When it gets cold, so do you. When it rains, you get wet. I've been in every state in this beautiful country. No one sees the country like a biker.

You and I rode to Yosemite the summer after you graduated from high school. We felt the spray coming off Halfdome and smelled pine so thick in the air you could cut it with a knife. We were chased by a bear in Yellowstone and helped butcher an elk near the Tetons.

Warm and dry. Somehow the reality isn't quite as good as the anticipation. The roaring in my heart now replaces the roaring of the wind.

How will I deal with your burial? How will I listen to taps and receive the flag those scrubbed young men in their spit-shined shoes will present to me? It took every bit of my self-control not to bawl like a baby when I went on burial detail so many years ago. That's what they did to brand new second lieutenants; they made them tough by sending them to people who'd just lost the reason they lived. "The President and the Secretary of the Army wish to convey their deepest regrets...." The toughest, red-neck bully in the world would melt into a sobbing mess right in front of my eyes. I had to be the post they clung to—I had to be strong, so they could be weak. God, I hated that job. And now I get to be the dad instead of the soldier.

Well, sleep isn't gonna to happen; too many ghosts running around behind my eyelids. So, I might as well see what that watering hole up the street has to offer. If I'm lucky, they'll have a decent burger and some cold beer.

Yep. The burger is somewhere between a gut bomb and OK. Maybe a bit more toward the OK side—it could have been a lot worse—only two other people in there besides the cute barmaid who took my order. I could tell she wanted to talk, but one glance into my eyes, and she left me alone.

Grief has a look, unique from all the others. Anyone who's been there will understand. It's like looking out at a different universe through a hole that happens to be your eyes. Things happen, but they don't affect you since you aren't part of that universe anyway. She left me alone to my thoughts, and I truly appreciated it. I'll have to go back someday and tell her thanks.

    I tossed and turned that night, staring at the reflection of the Vacancy light, still blinking on and off in the office. I would wake up periodically, which told me I had actually gotten to sleep for a while. When I saw the first light of dawn creeping over the hills behind the motel, I was up and into the wind. The rain had stopped last night sometime. The clouds were gone, and the world had done its scrubbed thing. Another time, another place, I would be in heaven. Today, I am one day away from being home.

    Mile after mile clicked by. Hour after hour. Things started to look familiar: a Cracker Barrel we'd eaten at after that long ride back from the redwoods, a bar we'd gotten thrown out of when the owner, an ex-marine, took exception to our dumb marine jokes. I guess they were a little too close to home.

    The exit to home came up like a bad dream, the kind you wake up from really glad it's a dream. But this was no dream. I took the exit ramp and waited for the light at the bottom. The light changed, and I turned, only fifteen more miles to home.

    They were a blur. I'd ridden them so many times I didn't have to think about it. My bike knew the way on autopilot. I stopped at the top of the last hill. The valley where our house had been since you were born stretched out in front of me. Dusk filled the sky with burnished pinks and grays. Lights were coming on in the houses, along with Buck's damned night light in front of his barn. It shines right into my bedroom window, and nothing I could say or do would get him to turn it off. Griff's horses were grazing in the pasture next to his house. My dogs started barking at a coyote calling to his family across the valley.

There is no counting the times you and I stopped here at just this time of day to enjoy the ride for a few minutes longer, neither one of us ready for the magic of it to end. Finally, the night would arrive, and the lights would draw us forward like moths to the flame.

"C'mon, Bill," I said, brushing off the rear seat and lowering the foot pegs. "Let's ride this last little bit together."

Get Them OFF!

The car drove by slowly, an elderly female driver staring at me as she negotiated the turn in front of my parents' house. I realized I was stark naked, standing outside in a Princeton suburb, taking a shower from the end of a garden hose.

Let me explain.

I grew up with a German Shepherd dog named Thunder. He tolerated my excesses, and I tolerated his. By the time I came home from Vietnam, he had grown old.

When Mom and Dad moved into this house, Dad built a pen for Thunder adjoining the house, complete with rounded river rock for Thunder's old feet. He also made a doggie door that went from the pen into the crawl space under the house so Thunder could stay warm and dry in the damp New Jersey winters. Then, as Thunder aged, Dad added a ramp outside and steps inside so Thunder could climb in and out more easily on his failing rear legs.

Our vet put Thunder to sleep one Christmas season while the whole family held his paws and watched his eyes go wide. My brother, sister, and I had grown up with Thunder. He had accompanied us on camping trips, boat outings, and summers at our grandparents' lake house. Mom and Dad thought we should be part of Thunder's departure from the here and now, so as he slowly declined in health that last year, they had nursed him and kept him alive. We buried him that afternoon. I dug his grave through the frozen New Jersey soil, and Mom planted a dogwood tree in the hole as we filled it in. Mom always liked puns. Dad never wanted another dog. I guess it hurt too much to bury his old friend.

On a hot day the following summer, I had to get into Mom and Dad's house. Both my parents were at work, and the doors were locked. Being a young man then, still skinny from the Army, I crawled into the crawl space through Thunder's doggie door. Given its name, I'm not sure you should enter a crawl space in any other manner. Sunlight passing through the plastic doggie door gave scant illumination to the area. After a few moments, my eyes adjusted. In one corner, a worn pad lay where Thunder used to sleep. Dirty grit and hair that Thunder had tracked in and shed covered the floor. Thunder's area was about eight feet square with a four-foot ceiling. Cool air filled the crawl space, which felt great since I had worked up a sweat wiggling through the doggie door.

Dad had built a partition between Thunder's area and the rest of the crawl space. The other end of the crawl space, about ten feet away, opened into the main basement area, which had access to the rest of the house. Dad had framed the partition with two-by-fours—he made everything out of two-by-fours. Onto the frame, he had attached the same dog fencing he used to encircle Thunder's pen. At one end of the partition, he had fabricated an access door. He used it to enter Thunder's area from the crawl space to clean it several times a year with his shop vac. It had hinges and a latch—both on the other side of the partition from where I kneeled. I could see them, but I couldn't quite reach either one.

By stretching the wire of the rectangular holes in the fencing, I worked my fingers around the two-by-fours and released the latch, then crawled into the basement side of the crawl space and made my way through Mother's gardening pots, rolls of carpet remnants, and boxes of her treasured junk.

Just before I jumped down into the people's part of the basement, I heard a soft hiss. I looked around for the source but couldn't see anything in the basement's darkness. So, after another pause to examine the area again, I climbed into the basement proper, then went up the stairs to the kitchen.

I glanced down at my arms, and ... I looked again. My arms were black, and the skin was *moving*. My arms were covered entirely with fleas—not a single bit of the skin visible, just my pink fingernails sticking through the black mass. The hiss I had heard was the sound of hundreds of thousands of ravenous fleas leaping onto the sweating, hairless arms of the animal crawling through their midst. It had been six months since Thunder died. I must have looked like a hot buffet to the starving insects.

For a moment, I had no idea what to do; then autopilot took over: *GET THEM OFF!* The command might as well have been shouted.

I ran out to the garage, where Mom and Dad had a hot water spigot with a hose. They used it when they washed Thunder. I grabbed the end of the hose, turned the faucet on *full hot,* and ran outside, pulling my clothes off as I went. I washed the fleas off, then grabbed the half-full bottle of flea shampoo next to the sink and washed again, from head to toe. Thank God Mom never threw anything out!

As I rinsed the soap off, the car with its elderly driver passed by. I picked up my soaking wet clothes and carried them down to the basement to the washing machine, where I deposited the dripping mess, added the rest of the bottle of flea shampoo, and started a wash cycle on HOT. I dressed in a pair of Dad's tennis shorts and one of his T-shirts, then went back outside to spray insecticide where I had washed.

Mom never did figure out the identity of the woman in the car. She was too embarrassed to go knocking on her neighbors' doors and explain the reason for her visit. She did make me a deal, though: "Promise never to do that again, and I will get the house bombed for fleas." The following weekend became Demise Days for the insects.

Gina

I tried to command myself to remember the war wasn't here, that these fir-covered mountains weren't hiding hard people with brown skin who wanted to kill me. Closing my eyes and inhaling the smells of the forest helped a little. It filled me with memories of pretty girls at the swimming hole, of my first .22 rifle lying on my bed for my twelfth birthday, and of picking out my very own puppy from the squealing pile between the hay bales.

Afghanistan still filled my consciousness. Every puff of wind and rustle of a leaf pulled me away from the peace I longed for—peace I had felt when I sat here so many years ago. You didn't stay alive in a combat zone by relaxing. Let your guard down for one second, and that second could be your last. The little sounds are so much more important than the big ones.

The temperature had dropped with the sun, chilling the still air among the ghosts and memories. Fragrances of damp earth, ferns, and cedar filled my campsite, so close to where I grew up. The fingers of ice crystals began their nightly metamorphosis, slowly growing across the puddle outside of my tent as if some invisible night creature were doodling on a canvas of water. The pale gray of dusk had almost finished changing into night.

This valley in central Washington was heaven on earth to a twelve-year-old boy with one pair of shoes that only got put on for Sundays and school.

"I'll name you Socks," I told the golden wiggling furball with four white feet as she tried to climb up the front of my shirt and lick my face.

She was a boxer mix and the best present a twelve-year-old could ever have. Socks became my constant companion. She slept next to me in my bed, walked with me to the school bus stop each morning, and waited for me when I returned in the afternoon. I saved her the choicest scraps from breakfast and dinner and sneaked her some of my meals when I didn't have anything else to feed her.

I've never seen a more natural hunter. Together explored this valley from the foggy river at the bottom to the snowcapped hills at the top. We'd hunt from the moment I got my shoes off after school until the sun crawled behind those cold rock walls. If we were lucky, I would bring home rabbits, a pheasant, or whatever critter was unfortunate enough to cross paths with us.

On those days when I returned with a full game bag, Socks and I would look forward gleefully to the ceremony of entering the house my grandfather built. I would swing open the front door and put the bag on the table, proud to contribute some tiny bit to my family's well-being, feeling every bit a man in a boy's skin.

Mom would come out of the kitchen, pushing back a lock of her graying, brown hair and wiping her hands on her apron before she hugged me. Her dresses always smelled of lemon and flour. Dad would shake his head and lament how poor the hunting would be next year since I cleaned out the hillsides of all the game. His wrinkled, leathery hands, now dark with age spots and swollen with arthritis, would lift out what critter I brought home and ask me where I found it and what it did. His eyes squeezed into sparkling slits with laugh lines that went all the way to his ears as he listened to the adventures Socks and I had that day, his ample belly wiggling with laughter that made his suspenders stretch even more.

Socks got all the parts we didn't want and sometimes some of my meal too when I figured she deserved more, crunching up the bones gleefully like rock candy.

We were a deadly pair. She would run through the woods roughly paralleling me, up and down the hills, through open forest, and down into stream beds thick with ferns and fallen branches. Every time I heard a growl, I knew she had found something. I would creep down through the blackberries and brambles until I saw where she was. She would never move. Once I moved into position, she would pounce on whatever she had found, and I would have one shot from that bolt-action, single-shot rifle. That was usually enough.

When you work for fifty cents an hour, a box of .22 shells gets mighty expensive. The summer I got that rifle, I worked and practiced and practiced and worked, spending every penny I made on shells. By the time fall came, I could shoot the walnuts off the tree in our backyard from a hundred and fifty feet. From then on, every critter had to be on the lookout, whether it walked, flew, or swam.

One day Socks discovered a porcupine. She had never seen a porcupine before. It waddled down a dry creek bed, as unafraid of Socks as a Sherman tank driver would be of a rifleman. Nothing had ever ignored Socks before. I think it hurt her feelings She growled and waited for me to come. I heard her, but I was stuck in a blackberry thicket. When I didn't show up for a while, she growled again, louder this time—damned blackberries! I didn't know what had happened when I heard her yelp, so I tore loose from those thorns and left some skin behind.

By the time I found her, the porcupine had fled into its den under a log, leaving Socks bristling with quills from one side of her face to the other. After that first attack, she must have hurt, and she hadn't expected to hurt. So she did what all hunters do—she attacked again and again. She had quills in her mouth, in her paws, up her nose—one even went through her left eye. She was almost blind, in pain, and running in circles, pawing at her face with her mouth wide open trying to dislodge the quills.

I rolled her up in my jacket to quiet her down and keep her from doing any more damage while considering my options. She couldn't walk, and we were a good ten miles from anything.

"Socks, what were ya thinking?"

She watched me with her good eye, trusting me to find a way of fixing what was wrong.

Nothing else to do but carry her. She weighed every bit of forty-five pounds, and I weighed maybe a hundred, soaking wet. I slung my rifle across my back with the barrel pointing down, then leaned over and gently pulled her over my head onto my shoulders. With her paws in both hands, somehow I got to my feet and began the long walk down to Doc Johnson, Chambersville's vet.

It took me five hours to reach town, walking up and down those hills with Socks on my back. I tried to walk as smoothly as possible so I wouldn't bounce her, but in all that time, she didn't move or wiggle around. Sometimes she would whimper softly, but nothing else, even when I would stumble on a rock or have to jump across a stream.

By the time we reached his office, Doc Johnson was closing up for the day. He was a large man, tall and wide. I guess that explained why he always wore suspenders and a belt. His long hair and bushy eyebrows were snow white. Add a cherry nose and red cheeks, and you'd be close. But his eyes I remember most of all. He had hazel eyes that were always smiling—eyes so big and friendly that you could get lost in them and forget what he just said.

"So Socks discovered porcupines, did she?" he asked, looking her over. "Come on in. Let's get 'er cleaned up."

He unlocked the door he had just locked, and I followed his huge, lumbering body, carrying Socks into the back. We worked on her for almost two hours before the last quill hit the pan. He put those bloody quills in a pill bottle for me as a souvenir, then gave me a second bottle full of antibiotics for the infection that was sure to come.

"I don't think 'er eye's gonna make it, David. That quill went through both sides an' tore the eyeball. I've fixed it as best I can, but I don't wanna get yer hopes up. She may have ta learn to hunt with only one eye."

I counted those damned quills when I got home. That porcupine had planted over five hundred into Socks.

I worked for the doc all summer, cleaning cages and walking dogs to pay for Socks's treatment. We got to be pretty good friends. He would let me help him as he fixed people's dogs, cats, and farm animals—said I had a natural talent for it.

Socks's eye never did work again, but that didn't stop her—I don't think it even slowed her down much. However, one thing did change that summer. Socks never got over her hatred for those slow-moving, quill-covered children of Satan. I could tell every time she found one. She had a "porcupine" bark, separate and unique from all her other barks. She never got stuck with another quill, but she never tired of terrorizing those poor animals.

A couple of years later, she figured out how to kill them without getting stuck. She would wait until they would begin to climb over a log or a rock. A gap would appear between the porcupine and the ground. She would reach underneath using her paw like a hand and flip them over, exposing their unprotected belly. Never saw another porcupine in our valley after that.

She also loved to chase things that would run from her. Deer were her absolute favorite. We were walking across an old cornfield, long gone fallow, when a young doe jumped up from where she had been sleeping and took off toward the tree line. Socks went after her just as quickly. They ran across the field, the doe weaving and cutting as Socks got from one side of her to the other. They almost made it to the tree line when the doe made one more cut and ran dead into a fence post, paying too much attention to Socks instead of where she was going. By the time I got to them, the doe had died of a broken neck.

Socks pushed the doe hopefully with her nose. Finally, she looked up at me as if asking, "Why doesn't she get up? I wanna play some more."

I thought about what to do. We were nowhere near deer hunting season. Still, the doe was dead, and no one living in the country ever lets food go to waste. So I gutted her and gave the heart and kidneys to Socks as the hunter's prize. I put the liver in my game bag, wrapped in my T-shirt, cut off her head and feet to lower the weight, then slung the carcass over my shoulders.

"It's a good thing she's a yearling, Socks," I said as she ate the parts I had given her. "We woulda had ta make two or three trips if she'd been full-growed."

Even dressed out, that deer weighed eighty pounds or more. We began the long walk back to Grandpa's house.

I don't know how game wardens know to drive down a certain road at a certain time. The state must test for it when people apply for that job. I've walked down that same logging road a hundred times and have never seen another living soul. But today, of all days, there he came.

He pulled up to me with that doe across my shoulders, took out his handkerchief, and wiped the sweat off his flushed forehead. The small amount of hair he had left made a white horseshoe around the top. His red flannel shirt had dark sweat stains under both arms and down his chest. Why a fat old man would wear a flannel shirt, long johns, long pants, and suspenders on a hot day like this was beyond me.

"Little early for deer, David," he said, pocketing his handkerchief.

"Yeah, I know. Socks ran 'er into a fence post—broke 'er neck. I couldn't leave 'er to waste."

"Well, put her in the back and get in. You too, Socks."

I climbed into the passenger seat, Socks jumped onto my lap, and the two of us sat there with our heads down, feeling like criminals.

He picked up my rifle and smelled the chamber. It hadn't been fired since I cleaned it the night before. He handed me back my rifle and turned his old truck around.

As he pulled into the dirt driveway that led up to Grandpa's house, all Dad's hounds began sounding off like they had treed the biggest coon of all time. The chickens ran every which way when he stopped, clucking their displeasure. Mom came through the doorway, her apron tied around her waist and some flour on her forehead.

"Afternoon, Annalee," the warden said to her, touching the brim of his dirty old game warden hat. The Department of Natural Resources seal on the front had become so faded and grimy you could barely make it out. He'd been the game warden around here since before I was born.

"Hi, Chester," she said, smiling. "What's he done now?" She gave me the lifted eyebrow look only mothers ever master.

"Found 'im up on the 35 with that doe across his shoulders." He pointed into the back of his truck. "Said Socks ran her into a fence post, and she broke her neck. Thought he could use a lift home. That doe weighs almost as much as he does."

She laughed at that. "Well, thanks for helping, Chester. I think David would love ta give ya a hind quarter for yer trouble." She raised that eyebrow at me again.

"You bet, Mr. Quintard," I swallowed, jumping up and pulling out my knife.

He motioned for me to stop, then mopped his forehead again and looked out across the valley for a minute before he answered Mom.

"I'd love ta have some venison for dinner, Annalee, no doubt, but I can't accept it. The law is pretty clear about that."

It took a while for him to say all those words. He puffed a lot between words like he was having trouble catching his breath. I stood by the tailgate of his truck with my knife in my hand, kind of mesmerized by the wiggling of his triple chin when he talked. He got out of the truck and stared at the doe for a couple of minutes while he decided what to do.

"I'm sure the women's shelter would be happy for some venison. I'll be goin' right past there on my way home. Whenever I find clean 'roadkill,' they jus' turn inside out when I drop it off for 'em."

I cut him out a full hind quarter and threw in the back strap and liver along with it. Those poor kids who lived with their mothers in that shelter were skin and bones when they came to school. Mom gave him some onions, carrots, and potatoes from her garden to go along with it. We may have been poor, but we were never hungry and didn't mind sharing with people in need.

When I turned fourteen, a couple of buddies and I decided to spend the weekend camping next to the river. We brought our rifles, dogs, and coolers full of pop and food. We had just settled in for an evening of hot dogs and ghost stories when a guy we'd never seen before came running into our campsite. He didn't have a jacket or hat on and was breathing hard. He looked around with crazy eyes and fought for breath as he leaned over and put his hands on his knees.

"Have you guys seen a woman?" he managed to ask.

"A woman?" I looked at my friends. "Ain't no one up here but us. An' we been here all afternoon."

"What'd she look like, mister?" Larry asked.

"I don't know, kinda tall, dark hair, pretty in a strange way. She had a red-and-blue-flowered dress on. She wasn't young, but then she wasn't old either. I've been talking to 'er for a couple a hours down by the shore." He looked around again, sighed, then started walking back the way he'd come.

"Do ya know which way she headed, mister?" Jack, my other friend, called out to him.

"If I knew that, why would I be talking to you guys?" he snapped.

He turned on his heel angrily, took a few steps back toward the river, then stopped and turned around.

"I'm sorry, kids," he apologized. "I went inta the woods to take a leak n' when I came back she was gone. I been searching for 'er for the last hour. Haven't found hide nor hair of 'er. It's like she vanished inta the river. Even with that big moon up there, I couldn't see her or even footprints showing which direction she'd gone."

He sat down next to our fire as he caught his breath, staring into the flames. I examined him more closely. He looked to be in his mid-twenties, clean-shaven, with red hair in a flat-top haircut. His short-sleeved shirt and slacks were pressed and probably expensive. His arms bulged with muscles that matched his broad chest and slim waist.

"Where ya from, mister?" I asked. "We don't get many strangers up here."

"Owens Ford, about forty miles south a here. I wanted to get away from my folks and think about things for a while. Havin' a little trouble at home. So I decided to come up here and try to figure out what to do. I had just set up camp when she came walking in."

"Did she say where she was from?" Larry asked. "We might know 'er."

"No, she didn't say much about herself. I think that's what I liked most about her. She listened and listened.

Sometimes she would ask a question. But mostly, she let me talk."

I didn't know any females like *that*. All the girls I knew were all about them.

"You want some help searching for 'er, mister? Did she tell you 'er name?" We started to get up.

"No. Never mind," he said, getting up also. "I think I'll go home. She'll be all right. The funny thing is, I believe I've figured out what to do. About the time I had ta go pee, the answer came as clearly as if someone spoke it. When I come back, she was gone."

He walked away into the night, and none of us ever saw him again. However, Larry, Jack, and I never forgot the muscled man who came out of the night trying to find the mysterious woman who showed him the way. Each time we camped on that same spot, we made up stories about him suddenly appearing and bringing that woman with him. She would have wet stringy hair and be covered with weeds from the river and blood on her hands. Pop changed into beers. Girls started to accompany us on the campouts. Our bicycles became dirt motorcycles, then four-wheel-drive trucks. The woman became a ghost from a ghastly murder, searching for her murderer among the visitors to the river. Our stories of her would terrify the girls and make them snuggle closer while they looked out fearfully into the dark forest.

I grew up, and Socks grew old. By the time I graduated from high school, she was slowing down. Her puppies had come and gone. Doc Johnson spayed her after the last litter, and I helped him do it. We'd done so many operations together on people's pets we didn't even have to talk while we were working.

That fall, I joined the Army. Mount St Helens, southwest of us, had erupted, and I couldn't wait to escape the dust and tourists who had descended on us. The Army accepted me into Medic training, then Airborne training, Ranger training, and finally Green Beret training. Somewhere along the way, Socks died. Maybe she gave up on me ever coming back home. Perhaps she had gotten as old as I felt now, after thirty years of black ops that never seemed to change anything, no matter whom or how many people we killed.

Chambersville had become very different from my childhood memories. I rode my new Harley, my retirement present to myself, down that twisting excuse for a road that led to town. The logging dried up when they made these hills a national monument. When the logging ended, the lumber mill closed, and so did most of Chambersville. Almost all the people moved away to somewhere they could earn a living, leaving their houses vacant and slowly decaying into dust. The people who remained were either waiting to die next to their memories or making a living off the tourists who descended on Chambersville every weekend and all summer.

I had stopped by Grandpa's house when I first arrived. Mom and Dad were both gone now, buried behind the house in the family cemetery. No one had lived in that house for years. I walked around inside, letting the memories of my childhood fill me for a while. I was born late in their lives, an unexpected gift after thinking children wouldn't be part of their time here on earth. I hadn't returned since they died.

Dad went first, laying his lungs on the altar of tobacco addiction like so many of his generation. Mom followed him three years later. She had been so sad for those three years. She never smoked, but I think she didn't want to live without him by her side. He was her childhood sweetheart. They grew up together, then old together. I believe he was waiting for her on the other side when she passed through.

The old cabinets in the kitchen, with their scuffed finish, had worn spots next to the handles from a lifetime of Mom's hands opening and closing them. I pulled open the drawer where she kept her aprons. She always wore one of these worn-out scraps of cloth wrapped around her waist while she cooked.

I picked one up and held it to my nose—nothing left of her but a faint mildew odor.

In my bedroom, up the stairs on the second floor, my old high school stuff was still hanging on the walls. The .22 rifle from my childhood stood in the corner. I picked it up, chuckling at how light and small it was. The rifles I used in the Army were much larger and heavier.

I pulled it up to my shoulder and sighted through the window at a squirrel sitting on a branch of the ancient walnut tree beside the house. The squirrel stared back at me without moving, then turned and scampered down the limb with a walnut in its mouth—a soft brown sheen of rust covered the barrel. I pulled out the cleaning kit, still under my bed, and went through the motions of putting a new coat of oil on my old friend.

I had continued paying the taxes on this property after Mom passed but had turned the electric service off long ago. After Mom's funeral, I drained all the pipes, then let the house sit here empty, not willing to release it to another family, not ready to let some strangers begin to replace my dusty old memories with their shiny new ones.

I put some more wood on the campfire. As near as I can figure, this is where Larry, Jack, and I had camped on those summer nights so long ago. The Harley made it down the old trail as if she'd done it a hundred times. Lots easier riding on it now that the rocks and roots were gone. I had busted my ass more than once on them on my bicycle.

When President Regan declared this area a national monument, a bunch of kids with shovels, chain saws, and pry bars made this trail by the river smooth and wide. Now it has become just another trail through the woods that only tourists use, going from one place where no one lives to another where it's much the same.

I got camp set up as night fell—a little lean-to with a poncho on top in case it rained with my tent protected by the lean-to. I had made shelters like this all over the world. When something works, you stick with it. Some people seem to love to get out in the woods so they can get cold and wet—like it is a necessary part of the "outdoor" experience. Warm and dry are fine for me. I've been wet and cold enough to last me for the rest of my life.

I remembered the guy we'd met on that night so long ago. I wonder if he'd ever found his answers. Then I thought about saying goodbye to my best friend in the world, Marley Butterhorn, six weeks ago. His friends knew him as "Doc."

I laughed as I realized I had also called Doc Johnson "Doc" when I helped him with his practice. No two people could be more different. Doc Johnson was a massive man with a heart of gold. My friend Doc in the Army was much smaller, maybe 5'8", 160 pounds, with sandy hair. If you passed him on the street, you wouldn't have given him a second glance—unless you'd seen his eyes. He had gray eyes. Some people think gray eyes are really light blue. Nope, not Doc's. His eyes were gray. Those eyes could be gentle and warm or cold as ice. While he kept you alive and laughing at your injuries, you'd never know he was one of the deadliest men in the Army. He had been my teammate in the Green Berets, my companion, my savior, and my best friend through the hell and high water of thirty years of war. My mind drifted back to six weeks ago when I said goodbye to him.

After Doc and I hugged for the last time, I threw my leg over that shiny new Harley. One touch of a button, and she began her comforting purr. As I pulled away, Doc snapped to attention and gave me a crisp salute. "Bittersweet" is not a strong enough word to describe the feelings I had at that moment: the end and the beginning—the end of my career as a Green Beret and the beginning of my life as a civilian. Doc disappeared behind a building along with thirty years of brotherhood, shared dangers, and lost friends.

I cruised up to the last stop sign before exiting the base. It was time to think about the future instead of the past. As I approached the guard shack, a full-face grin blossomed from ear to ear. There *are* worse ways to begin a new life. I had a beautiful new motorcycle between my legs. The temperature hovered around 80 degrees. The sky had that unique shade of blue it gets next to the ocean with some puffy white clouds drifting around up there. Three thousand miles away, my home in Washington State beckoned me. Between here and there, a fantastic country that I hadn't seen enough of in the past thirty years was waiting to be explored. What to do next could go on hold until tomorrow, next week, or even next month.

"I think I'll name you Socks," I said to the bike as we were waved past the guard shack and into my new life. Then we were away into the wind. Names don't have to make sense to anyone else.

The ride home took six weeks. I hadn't taken a single interstate or freeway if I could avoid it. Instead, I stopped at every little Podunk crossroads I passed and talked to the people I had been defending for thirty years. Along the way, I visited every VFW, American Legion, Vietnam Veteran's club, and National Cemetery I could find. What a great trip!

And now I'm sitting next to a campfire, still undecided about what to do next. The flames had burned down until they appeared to be individual spirits dancing on the logs as they consumed the wood. I stared into the fire for a few minutes, then decided I was ready. I reached into a hidden inner pocket in my leather jacket and took out a hand-rolled cigarette.

Doc had rolled this joint for me. He tucked it into the breast pocket of my motorcycle jacket as I got ready to leave. As he pulled up the zipper on the pocket, he said, "Sometime, somewhere, you will find the place to smoke this. When you do, ask a question, and you will find the answer."

I crawled into my tent, stretched out on my sleeping bag, and pondered Doc's statement. Only one question was important to me at this moment in my life: "What the hell am I supposed to do now?" So I asked it to the air inside the tent, then lit the end of the joint. The glowing tip had the appearance of an eye in the darkness. The jumping images of the campfire on the walls provided a kind of psychedelic illumination.

An owl hooted above my tent, so loud that the owl must have been on a branch only a foot away. I tensed, waiting for the shit storm. Whenever a big change was about to bring my life as I knew it down around my shoulders, an owl announced its arrival moments before the shit hit the fan. You laugh, but it has happened so often to me that I can't even hear an owl hoot in a movie without putting my head down, bracing for the blast—Hootie and the Blowhard—best friends forever.

"Hello, the camp," a voice said from down the hill.

Crap! Has to be a ranger, and me with this bomber just lit.

"Thanks for the warning, owl!" I grumbled. Pot might be legal in Washington State, but I was camped in a federal goddamned monument area.

I stubbed the joint out and crawled through the door, having tucked my .45 into the small of my back.

What I found wasn't what I expected. Instead of a ranger with an attitude, a middle-aged woman waited patiently while she clutched a thin gray jacket around herself like she was freezing to death. She had shoulder-length, auburn hair and a dark skirt that stopped at her knees.

"Can I warm up next to your campfire, please? I took a walk on this trail and lost track of time. Now the sun's gone down, and I'm miles from my car."

"Of course. Have a seat."

I dragged a log over to the fire for her and another one for me. I put a few more pieces of wood on the fire from what I had collected before dark.

She seemed a little ill at ease. I guess I didn't blame her. Here we are out in the middle of nowhere, and she's sitting next to a biker-lookin' guy who'd been God knows where doing God knows what.

"So, where do you live?" I asked, making conversation.

"I live here," she said, smiling for the first time. "I've lived here all my life. My name's Gina."

This time *I* studied *her*. She didn't remind me of anyone I knew. But time has a way of changing people. She still had the beauty that must have driven the young men crazy when she was young. She had to be forty-five or fifty now.

She pulled her thick hair back into a soft ponytail and tied it with a yellow ribbon at the back of her neck.

I guess I've changed too. Every time I stare at the person in the mirror, I have to study my face longer than the last time. Then slowly, I can see the young man that left home so many years ago. He's still there for now, but I wonder how much longer he will stay around and what I will do when he leaves for good.

"I used to live here, too," I said. "I guess there's a lot of people who can say that now."

She looked at *me* then and shrugged. "I don't remember you, but I don't remember a lot of things—been a few changes around here. Sometimes I feel like my world is dust. No matter how hard I try to pick some up and hold it in my hand, it slips through my fingers and drifts away."

She held her feet up to the fire. Her beat-up loafers had no socks and wouldn't have kept a mouse warm on a summer day.

I started talking. I don't know why. I told her about my childhood and growing up in Chambersville, about my time in the Army, about the good men who had died in my arms as I tried to fix them up, about the children with blown-off arms and legs who believed the big American soldier could save their lives while they looked at me with those huge dark eyes and died, about the babies women would throw into our trucks so we would take them back to the States and give them a chance they would never have at home. I talked about things I had promised myself I would never talk about. I even talked about Socks and how I was away fighting a war when she died.

I went back into the tent and retrieved the joint Doc gave me. I sat down by the fire and lit the end. The two of us passed it back and forth until I tossed the roach into the fire.

She leaned across my chest and kissed me.

"Thanks for going," she said. "There're a lot of men who are alive because you were there to plug the holes in them. You may remember the ones you lost, but you need to remember the ones you didn't. Now those men have wives and children who think the world of them, and you're the reason why. Those children you watched die were a small fraction of the ones you saved. They will never forget the tough American soldier who saved them when no one else would."

Then she took my hand and led me into the tent. The rest is kind of a blur, but I smile every time I think about it, my first and last night with the woman who healed my soul.

You might think it was weird having sex with a woman who had shown up on the side of a trail on a chilly night in October. Well, it wasn't like that. We didn't have sex. I don't know what we had. I can't remember what happened, and I've tried to remember it a thousand times. All I remember is how great I felt when we were done. Call it an out-of-body experience. Call it a healing. Call it great pot. Call it whatever you want, but I have no idea what she did.

She was gone when I awoke. I looked around the campsite, but there weren't even footprints in the dust from where I knew she'd walked. She might as well have been a ghost. What I do remember is never having felt so healthy, so alive, so in tune with everything around me as I did when I crawled out of that tent. I had been reborn and couldn't wait to start discovering what my new life was all about.

I packed the camp onto Socks, and we rode back to Grandpa's house. I got a pad of paper from the desk in my room and started inventorying what I would need to buy to begin fixing up the house. I walked outside, studying the sagging porch, faded paint, and gutterless eaves.

"Better see what tools are left in Dad's workshop," I muttered, walking around the house, then into the old barn.

I heard a noise from the back. I pulled my .45 out as I crept around some old bales of hay. There, between two bales, a litter of puppies and a mother who looked about half-starved to death stared back at me.

"Well, hello there, Mom. Who do you have here?"

A golden puppy crawled over to my boot and started to climb up, lost her balance, and splayed all four white feet up in the air. Then, she wiggled around and started up again. I reached down and picked her up. "I will call you Gina."

Paradise

It was falling through the Between that started my second life. The fall lasted perhaps three seconds after my apartment and friends vanished. In retrospect, I wished I hadn't screamed and clawed at nothing for the entire three seconds of falling through what looked like a glowing cotton ball, but when a dirt floor hits you in the face, you don't have a lot of options.

I looked up from the floor, the scream fading from my still open mouth—into the eyes of a rugged-looking, handsome young man, who appeared as shocked as me that I was in front of him. I sat up and turned around in panic. Dirt from the floor tasted bitter in my mouth. I spat it out and raised my hand to my face. Sore—my cheek was already sore, and I could feel it beginning to swell. I was in the middle of the same pattern my friends and I had drawn on the floor of my apartment in Chicago. But instead of my friends sitting around the pattern, four other young people I had never seen before sat in the same places my friends had been.

"Who are you?" I asked the man in front of me too loudly, trying to keep the hysteria out of my voice. "Where the hell am I?"

He looked at me, then at the other people around the pattern, as though asking them if they understood what I had said. Finally, he turned back to me and said something in a language I had never heard before. When he saw I was as baffled as he'd been, he asked me tentatively in Hebrew, "Who are you?"

"That's Hebrew," I thought. "He speaks *Hebrew*!" My mind still reeled from falling through the pattern. It took me a moment to shift mental gears into Hebrew.

"My name is Susannah," I told him.

The reality began to sink in. "Holy crap!" I thought with dismay. "It *worked*!"

Five minutes earlier.

"Joe! Are you ready?" Reid asked him, sounding a little irritated. Joe was acting like he didn't want to do this.

"Yeah. I guess so." Joe looked around again for some way to escape. In resignation, he sat down on a kitchen chair and announced, "I can't."

"What!" I asked in disbelief. "You're kidding, right? We've been at this for seven months, practicing every weekend, and tonight, the night when everything is ready, you '*Can't?*'" By the time I finished, my voice dripped sarcasm.

"That's right, Susannah, I can't." Joe's voice cracked as he said it. He looked at me in angry defiance. "You know what? I'll go farther than that: I *won't*!" He got up from the chair, his face red with anger, and began to pull on his jacket.

"Screw that!" I said, getting up. "If you won't do it, I will! You do my part, and I'll do yours. Do you think you can say my words? Is that asking too much?"

Joe looked back and forth between me, the pattern on the floor, and the other three students. He sighed in defeat and took off his jacket. "Yeah, I can do your part."

I watched him sit on the floor where I had been a moment ago. I tried to suppress the misgivings that were screaming at me from the inside of my big mouth: "What if this worked?" "Do you know what you're doing?"

I looked around one last time, pretending confidence I sure didn't feel, then took a deep breath—too late to back out now. My subconscious gave a malicious snort. "OK. I'm ready. Let's do it."

Everyone settled into their well-rehearsed tasks.

"Oh, hell," I thought, dismissing my fears with a nervous grin. "What am I worried about? This'll never work."

All of us are archeology graduate students working on our PhDs at the University of Chicago. I am the redhead of the group and also the athlete. I inherited my mother's good looks. To make some money one summer while an undergraduate at Emory University, I posed for Sports Illustrated Magazine's Swimsuit edition. They liked my long red hair and runner's body. Unlike most of my brainless female peers in the magazine, my idea of fun is running in the Chicago Marathon.

Reid, on the other hand, has never taken a fast step on purpose in his whole life. Short, round, clean-shaven with acne scars and already losing his sandy brown hair, his incredible mind made up for his unsavory appearance.

Joe is a mixed bag. He looks like he could be athletic, but I've never seen him move faster than a walk unless he was escaping from the path of an oncoming CTA bus. He has a short brown goatee and a short, military-looking crewcut. Sometimes he amazes me with his insight, and other times he baffles me with his stupidity.

Brian is the person closest to someone I would like as a boyfriend. He laughs a lot, always has kind words, knows when to shut up, and likes to lift weights. He keeps his blonde hair combed and is very proud of his soul patch.

We have one mystery person in our group—Jamie. She speaks fluent English with an accent I've never heard before. English sounds almost musical when she speaks it. She has brown skin, deep black hair, green eyes, and brilliant white teeth. Her teeth are so white they look artificial. She never talks about herself or where she originated from. I have tried to get her to open up about her past, but she just smiles and returns to work. I think she might come from a Persian Gulf country. With how some of those countries treat their women, I don't blame her for not wanting to talk about it.

Last summer, our second summer in graduate school, our advisor, Professor James, organized a dig at the Dead Sea in Israel. Professor James had a friend, a professor at American University in Tel Aviv. His friend had gotten us permission from the Israeli Department of Antiquities to participate in the dig.

We'd been turning up boring bits of pottery from around the birth of Christ and even several metal artifacts, but nothing exciting.

Ninety-nine percent of an archeologist's efforts were routine: dig-brush-identify-notate-preserve. Repeat until a square meter was excavated to a specified depth, then continue to the next square.

We almost always worked in the early morning and late afternoon because the middle of the day was so damned hot—heat that just overwhelmed everything else we did.

One afternoon we were lying under the canopy we used to escape from the blistering sun outside. Jamie came stumbling in, all glassy-eyed, mumbling in her odd accent that she'd found it, found the way to Paradise, then she'd passed out.

Since I had been an EMT on an ambulance crew for a while, I doubled as our team's Med-Tech. I checked Jamie out. Jamie's pulse was slightly high, but her temperature and respirations were normal. I decided she was just dehydrated. This happened a lot, the Dead Sea area being so hot and dry.

We carried Jamie to bed. I kicked everyone else out of our sleeping tent, undressed her, and started a saline IV drip. I figured she'd just been out in the sun too long and needed some rest and fluids. Jamie was out for the rest of the day and all night. I slept beside her so I could check her every couple of hours.

She awoke just as everyone got up for breakfast. She sat bolt upright in bed and shouted, "Paradise!"

That got everyone's attention – the men because I had put her to bed dressed in just a thin sleep shirt and underwear; the women because Jamie hadn't said twenty words that whole summer. We weren't sure if her statement was a dream, a promise, or a come-on.

As it turned out, it was kind of all three. Jamie had found a scroll that described a parallel universe named Paradise. It had no pollution, no wars, no lawyers, no politicians, and no police. Everyone just got along, worked together, and grew in peace. So the name "Paradise" seemed appropriate. The best part of the scroll was that, in addition to a description of Paradise, it included step-by-step instructions on how to open a portal to move someone from this universe to Paradise.

We were sure Professor James would either dissolve in laughter and compliment us on the quality of our joke or claim the find as his, and we'd never see the scroll again. So the five of us decided to break the laws of Israel as well as the laws of archeology. We decided to keep the scroll a secret and smuggle it back to Chicago to try it out. The portal ceremony required four people to hold open the portal, one for each dimension, while the fifth passed through. But we needed something called the Center of the Universe, whatever that was. It had to be in the middle of the pattern described in the scroll.

"Was there anything else in the jar?" I asked Jamie, looking over the scroll one more time.

"Not that I saw."

"Could you show us where you found it?" Reid asked.

Jamie led us up the hillside to the cave she'd unearthed. We wiggled through the opening into a small room. My head brushed the ceiling. Joe and Brian had to hunch down to stand. Against the far wall, we saw a single clay pot. Reid shined his flashlight into it.

"Nothing else in it but this little rock."

He examined it—just a piece of rock, kind of gray with beige streaks running through it, about the size of a squished golf ball. Reid gave it to Brian. "What do you make of this?"

Brian had a dual major: archeology and geology.

"It's igneous, but without doing a radiometric dating, I have no idea how old it is." Brian turned it over. "Hey, look at this." He handed it back to Reid and pointed to one facet. A little circle had been scratched into the stone with lines extending out from it.

When we returned to Chicago in September, we drew straws to see who the passenger would be, and Joe won (or lost, depending on how you looked at it). After that, the rest of us had specific parts of the ceremony that had to be practiced until we got them perfect.

The words were all in primitive Hebrew. Our time in Israel at the dig served us well. Before our trip, we had taken a crash course in Hebrew. For the whole time at the dig, we spoke Hebrew whenever we talked to the Israelis who worked in the next camp. Those conversations were great practice in our preparation for the ceremony.

After six months of spending each weekend doing rehearsals, we figured we had it down. Tonight was the night. It was 10:21 P.M. The alarm on my cell phone went off, announcing, "Send Joe through!"

The sun and earth were in the correct orientation to Aries, which happens just once every year. The lines were drawn, the candles lit, everyone was in their place, and the words said. All that remained was for me to step into the center of the pattern and see what happened. I looked at Joe with disdain, then around at my other three friends one more time. Finally, I took a deep breath, steeled myself for the unknown, and stepped into the pattern's center.

Nothing happened.

"Bummer," Jamie said, sighing in disappointment. "All that work and not even a wiggle in the air."

"Wait a minute," Reid told us. "Where's that little rock we found in the jar with the scroll?"

"I have it right here." Brian pulled it out of his pocket. "I wondered if we would need it. I just finished trying to date it, but it didn't work." Brian held up the rock for everyone to see. "The ratio of uranium-238 to lead-206 indicates this little pebble is older than Earth, by about three times, which would mean it would have been created about the time of the Big Bang." He laughed. "The damned undergrads must have knocked the spectrometer out of calibration again."

"Put it in the middle of the pattern," Jamie told him.

After Brian placed the rock, Reid told everyone, "Let's say the words again. I think we still have time before we lose the planetary window."

Everyone said the words in the proper order. I stepped into the pattern again, and—the world melted around me. Three seconds later, I flopped on the floor, cheek first, in front of four strangers.

The man across from me asked in Hebrew, "Why are you here?"

My mind still reeled from my fall. After I figured out how to say it in Hebrew, I told him, "I'm searching for Paradise?"

I could see they didn't understand. After my fourth attempt at explaining my mission, I saw the shock in his violet eyes for a split second. Then, slowly, his shock turned into a rueful smile and a chuckle, which grew and grew until tears flooded his face. I looked at the rest of the people. They were just staring at me until, one by one, each one joined in the laughter.

I began to get pissed off. I was about to cry, and that pissed me off even more—I hate women who cry! My cheek hurt where it had hit the floor. I didn't have a clue where I was or how I would get back to Chicago. I didn't know these people, and they were *laughing* at me.

"What's so *goddamned* funny?" I demanded.

He got control of his laughter enough to stammer, "So are we!"

The Longest Ride

"Man, what a downpour!" I shouted to the guy sharing the underpass with me. "Do you think it'll last long?"

He looked out at the maelstrom going on all around us. "It'll be at least an hour before it's clear enough to ride safely." He held out a pack of cigarettes. "Here, have a smoke and relax."

We both leaned back on our bikes and watched the smoke get blown away by the rooster tails of the cars passing in the rain.

He looked over at me during a lull in the traffic. "Where you goin' in such a hurry? Not many things worth getting killed over. Gettin' down the road ain't one of 'em."

How could I describe what was going on inside of me? Lisa and I coming so close to breaking up, getting different places, and trying to learn how to live without one another. Six months of pretending we were happy with idiots we didn't even like. Then her phone call last night. I'm miserable too, baby. Only one more hour until I can tell you to your face all the things I tried to say to you last night.

I tried to tell the guy all about Lisa, about what had happened to us, but the wet noise of the cars passing us kept drowning out my words. So finally, I gave up. We just sat there pondering our private thoughts.

How many times does life ever give someone a second chance? I figured I was about due. I lost my folks when I was a kid. My sister half-assed raised me when she wasn't partying or passed out. The army in 1968 was an escape, maybe a dumb escape, but at least I was on my own. Nam in '70 was pretty quiet until that RPG hit my truck. At least I got a short tour. After lots of jobs and many women, I woke up one morning with Lisa. She moved in, and suddenly it was a year later. We were married, and she was pregnant. That was almost twenty years ago, twenty good, solid years. She taught me how to be a father to our children. I taught her how to ride her motorcycle. We built hers in the living room one winter. We lived through twenty years of fun, love, and hard work. Then it all started going sour. I still don't know why. Neither one of us did. Finally, she left. It wasn't after a fight. It wasn't after anything. I came home, and she was gone. She'd left a note on the kitchen table that just said: "I love you. Good-bye." That was all until her phone call last night.

The rain was coming down even harder than before. The last remnant of daylight faded from the sky as I watched.

"I'm going," I said to the guy.

He looked down and shook his head. "Good luck, bro, but I think you're makin' a big mistake." He watched me pull out my kick starter pedal and bring the cylinder up to the compression stroke. Then, he decided to try one more time. "If you gotta go, how's about we just hit the next exit ramp and find a bar to hole up in until this passes? Come on; I'll buy the first round. Nothin' I hate more than buryin' good people when there are so many people runnin' around that deserve it."

"Sorry, man," I told him. "I gotta go. I'd drive across Hell itself to get home tonight."

He clenched my hand in his and looked me straight in the eye. "Ride free, bother. I hope she's worth it. Be careful."

I got out into traffic all right. Everyone was being really careful. After five minutes, I felt a tell-tale trickle of water slowly wind down between my legs. *I bet the people who design rain suits laugh whenever it rains. At least I can't get any wetter. Hard to believe, but I think it's coming down even harder. When those eighteen-wheelers go by, it's like getting hit with a fire hose.*

"Hey, God, you can do better than this!" I called out, laughing. "How about some hail? Freezing rain would be nice. You did frogs for Moses. I figure I'm good for, say, earthworms, or at least some two-day-old roadkill."

Straighten up, man. I scolded myself. *Gettin' kind of nutso. Lettin' this rain get to me. Hey, maybe this isn't rain at all. Perhaps it's a bunch of demons ahead of me with water pellet machine guns.*

"Hey, you guys, the M-60 ain't working. Why don't you try the .50 caliber? No, really, don't hold back. Don't you have a minigun or two up there? Come on, give me your best shot."

Brake lights! LOTS OF BRAKE LIGHTS! I CAN'T SEEEEE.!

I'm through. How did I get through? That station wagon was sliding right at me. Suddenly its tires bit, and it stopped. That's a sound I hate above all other sounds in the world: tires screaming on the pavement that end in a bike-killing crunch.

The rain is finally letting up. There's Lisa's exit. Oh, no! The throttle's stuck. I won't be able to make the off-ramp. Man! What's going on? Why can't I get this thing unstuck? My hands are stuck to the handlebars like they are glued to them. It's not cold enough for ice. What is going on? The brakes don't work. I can't pull the clutch. The gear shifter won't move. This bike is driving itself! No, Martha. Now is not the time to remind me about preventive maintenance. Martha. God, I haven't thought about her for years. Red hair and lonnnng legs. I hope she's happy wherever she ended up. Day dreamin'! Or is it night dreamin' being the sun went down hours ago? Hours ago! It's been hours since I missed Lisa's exit. This is like riding in a dream. Why haven't I run out of gas? I can go faster, but the bike always returns to the speed limit when I slow down. Uphill, downhill, fast, slow, no change in engine speed. It's almost like the bike's on a treadmill with a fan blowing wind in my face. When I go faster, it just speeds up the highway like hitting fast forward on a movie. I never hit anything, skid, or lose control. I don't think I could wreck even if I wanted to. Of course, I never really control anything but the speed. But speed is kind of fun when you can't crash.

I kept going faster and faster, seeing how crazy it could get. Imagine breaking the sound barrier in heavy traffic, blasting by cops, little old ladies in Cadillacs, dogs in the back of pickups. I got tired of it after a while. All that scurrying around was giving me a headache. The bike settled back into 55. I wasn't getting tired or hungry. I didn't have to pee.

Suddenly, it all started making sense. *I didn't make it through that accident. I'm dead. And this is the next world. I don't feel dead. I feel great! And I've still got my bike! And it goes fast! Far out! I didn't know it would be like this.*

The music started a little after that. It began by sounding like an ice cream truck bell. Then it became the Star-Spangled Banner. Then it was my high school football fight song. I was listening to a musical history of my childhood. By the time it got to Foghat, I was starting to get the hang of it. If I wanted it louder, I just thought it louder. If I wanted any particular song, all I had to do was start playing the music in my head, and it would suddenly start playing in the air around me. I could repeat a song. I could even play it backward if I could get the first couple of notes right.

When Slow Ride began, I had the volume up, way up. I was cookin' through Denver at about three hundred. I'd figured out I could go anywhere the Interstate System went, so I was making full use of it. I always wanted to see the Rocky Mountains. Out of the corner of my eye, I saw a demon on a very pretty knucklehead chopper. Harley-Davidson quit making the knucklehead motor in 1948. I wondered how he'd gotten the parts to build one. He leaned over, grinning, and gave me a big thumbs-up sign. Two more demons pulled in beside him in perfect formation with big grins on their faces. I'd always figured those guys liked Harleys and rock and roll.

What the Hell! Demons were better than no company at all. I leaned over to them and shouted, "Hey boys, let's party!"

I twisted the throttle, and off we went. Four hundred. Five hundred miles per hour. They stuck with me, but they weren't on autopilot. They actually had to drive that fast: damn quick reflexes, those demons. Then one of them wiped out. It was ugly. Bits of demon flesh spread over two or three miles along the road, and me without a skillet.

But it got me thinking. *If the demons dug going fast to killer rock and roll, maybe the head man would too. I wonder what he's like. All those old wives' tales and myths started coming up from my memory. I was going through Atlanta with The Devil Went Down to Georgia playing in the air. Charlie Daniels was smokin' the final few notes when the beginning of an idea came into my head. I just had to figure out how to get old Mr. Fire and Brimstone himself to ride with me. There was only one song that was the perfect song for this particular occasion and only one place to play it.*

Runnin' with the Devil with a full moon across Death Valley at midnight—no headlights, no traffic, going real fast. It took a while to set it up, but here we go. Not two bars into the song, I realized he was beside me. He had a twenty-foot-long, black pearl, supercharged Evolution Harley. Later that night, we entered Los Angeles.

We'd been taking turns choosing music, but I always chose the route. I'd chosen Hot Rod Lincoln as we were going up Grapevine. He'd chosen Burnin' Down the House as we went through Watts. I'd talked him into getting us off the freeway to cruise Hollyweird. I figured he'd have some warm memories from there. At Sunset and Vine, I began playing Dead Man's Curve. He looked at me questioningly for a second. Jan and Dean? Then comprehension dawned in his ol' poker playin' eyes. Me against him - all the way to Dead Man's Curve - winner take all. He smiled a little for the first time since our ride began.

The light turned green, and we were off. Damn, he was fast. We were tradin' back and forth for the lead, leavin' trails of sparks around the curves, going around people so fast we were gone before they knew we were there. He was fast, but my top end was unlimited. We must have been hitting Mach 3 coming into that hairpin. No force on earth could have kept us on that road. He looked over at me with a big grin as we went over the edge two thousand feet above the LA lights. Then he put on his afterburners and cut a vapor trail across the dawn. Prettiest thing I've ever seen.

Everything went black as I hit the bottom of the canyon.

"Wake up, man. You OK?"

I was looking into the face of the guy I'd shared the underpass with.

"Yeah, I guess so." I ran a hand through my hair and looked at it. No blood. Amazing. "What happened?"

"That station wagon over there damn near ran over you."

I sat up and looked at the station wagon. It was upside down and smoking. A woman was holding a child and walking around it.

"Man, I thought you were a goner. It happened right after you left the underpass."

I could see the disbelief in his eyes when I slowly got to my feet and shook my head to clear the cobwebs.

"Where's my bike?" I asked him, looking around.

"Over there, man." He indicated the other side of the station wagon.

I walked around the car and saw her lying on her side in the gravel at the side of the road. This wasn't good.

"I'll help ya get her up."

Together we put her up on two wheels. I pulled out the kickstand, leaned her onto it, and began to check out the damage. He was looking at me in disbelief as I walked around the bike, favoring my whole left side. *I'll worry about myself after I finish with the bike.*

He held out his hand. "Give me your keys, and I'll try to start it for ya."

"No thanks, man." I shook my head. "If she won't start for me, she won't start for anybody."

I pulled out the kickstart pedal and got ready to kick it through. Then I noticed the paint. The paint had changed. Not the road rash I had expected. It was black pearl with a laughing, red-eyed demon airbrushed on the tank. The demon was riding a long black chopper, flying across the dawn over LA underneath a full moon. I checked out the chrome and polished aluminum on the side she'd been lying on. It looked brand new. Better than new—it was flawless; even the worn-out tires had been replaced.

On the third kick, I got a cough. On the fifth, she caught. The rain had stopped, but the ground was still soaking wet. In the distance, I heard the sound of sirens coming to the accident. There were cars and people all over the road with stopped traffic behind us as far as I could see. My rear tire spun a little as I caught second.

"Crazy biker," the guy muttered. "Why would God waste a second chance on someone like that?"

It's Up to Jack

"Sam," I whispered, looking up, "it won't be long before we're finally together again. Did you wait for me, too?"

He died twelve years ago, right after our forty-first anniversary. His doctor detected it during a routine annual checkup. Then he had an MRI, a CT scan, and his pancreas removed. It didn't stop the cancer. The chemo and radiation did nothing but make him even sicker. Six weeks later, he died as I held him. My soulmate, my companion for forty-two years—stolen from me before our "golden years" had even begun.

Sometimes I still talked to him like he was in the room. Other times I just thought my end of our conversations. The older I got, the fuzzier that line became. In the years before our retirement, we planned the trip of our lifetime: Ireland, Paris, and New Zealand—the bucket list adventure that never happened. Instead, we sat together, holding hands in the oncologist's office, while he gave us Sam's death sentence.

Reality elbowed its way back into my thoughts.

Hospice, Sam. Remember hospice? Well, here's the thing. Tomorrow I'm moving to the same one you were in. This time it's my cancer that's winning. Chemo didn't help me, either. But I didn't fight very hard—certainly not as hard as you did. So, I guess I'm just ready to go. The doc says I can't live alone anymore. I suppose he's right. I can't even hold down Ensure. I'm leaking out of every orifice, and my clothes just hang on me like sacks.

Jack, the cat, jumped onto my lap, landing as gently as a feather. He was a gray and tan tortoiseshell, medium-hair cat—my companion since Sam died. My brother, Nathan, brought him over a week after the burial. That little, six-week-old fur ball was just what I needed to help me heal after losing Sam. Five years later, Nathan joined my husband on the other side, cut down by a stroke in the middle of the night.

And get this, Sam, remember how his brat kids fought over the largest piece from those apple pies I made? They descended on our house like locusts when I told them I had cancer. All they wanted to know was who got what. Now they're fighting over where the money from the house sale goes. I'm gonna give it all to cancer research instead of those bastards!

Jack got comfortable, a soft meow, his head on my thigh with a sigh of contentment. His purr engine started up. I refused to call him "my cat." He stayed with me because he wanted to.

"What would I have done without you, Jack? Without you depending on me for meals, water, and a clean litter box?"

OK, Sam—you put the idea in Nathan's head, didn't you? I missed you so much. And now hospice is waiting for me, and they don't allow pets.

Despair filled me again. I lost Sam, and now I'm losing Jack. I figured Jack had saved my life; yeah, saved it so I could die of cancer twelve years later.

I scratched Jack behind the ears, then between his eyes. His eyes became slits of pure kitty pleasure, and his purring went up about thirty decibels.

"What do you want to do, Jack" I whispered.

Why do people talk to their pets like they're people? What would they do if the poor thing actually answered:

"Gee, I'd like about a million mice to chase, all the Tender Vittles in the world, and catnip—lots of catnip."

Jack looked up at me and said "Meow" rather forcefully, as though he agreed with my thoughts.

I stood up, making him jump off my lap, and opened the front door, holding it for him. In the twelve years we'd been together, he had never wanted to go outside.

"Jack, do you want to leave? Maybe find another lonely old woman who needs you to help her through some personal nightmare."

Slowly Jack walked over to the open door and looked out, his head going from side to side and then up into the limbs of the trees next to my house. He turned to stare at me with his head cocked to one side as if he were asking, "Why are you doing this?"

"Go on, my friend. Make a life for yourself. It's a cat Heaven over there on the other side of that fence. There are more mice than you could ever eat in that wheat field."

Jack turned his back on the open door without a second look and jumped onto the seat of the maple ladder-back chair I'd gotten from Grandmother's estate. He curled up in the sun coming through the window, continuing the purr-solo he began in my lap.

I could take him to the shelter. They said they never put down unwanted pets. I still had the phone number on my cell phone. I hesitated, then pulled out the phone, my thumb hovering over the "call" button, when a knock sounded on my front door. Through the cut glass, garden-filled center of the door that Sam *HAD* to have when we built the house, I saw Stan Wilson, the real estate agent I had hired to sell the house.

"Hi, Stan," I said, opening the door. "What's up?" There would be plenty of time to make the call after Stan left.

"Good morning, Janice. I've got a family in the car. They want to take a look at your house. Is this a good time?"

I laughed, holding up my hand like it was an appointment calendar. "You're in luck. All I have today are good times."

"I've got to warn you," he whispered. "They have a little girl who doesn't speak."

"Can't or won't?"

"Don't know. What's the difference? I think she's adopted."

"Depends on the kid. But thanks for the warning. Bring 'em in."

Can't speak is one thing, but kids who won't speak have usually been abused. I looked past him to his car. I saw a man in the front passenger seat and a woman in the back.

Stan walked back out to the car and returned with the couple. A child dawdled behind them—maybe ten years old, with light brown skin and nappy hair—very different from her parents' white skin and blonde hair. The girl looked around at the trees and flowers. I still planted flowers in the raised beds in front of the house every year, just like Sam had done. It didn't seem like home without them.

"Come on, Marie." Her mother urged gently. "Keep up."

Before she walked up to join us on the porch, the little girl reached out to touch the firecracker petunias and stroked them almost lovingly.

"Those petunias were my husband's favorite," I told her.

She didn't respond to my comment or even acknowledge she had heard me.

Her parents went off with Stan to tour the house. Marie sat on the porch swing without saying a word, waiting for them to finish.

Stan called out to me. "Janice, could you come upstairs for a second? They have a question."

Stairs were a lot of work for me these days, even when I didn't fill my diaper as I struggled up them. I found them in the master bathroom.

"What's the history of this tub?" the woman asked.

I had to catch my breath before I could answer. "Sam bought it from a contractor tearing down another farmhouse about a mile from here. He told me the tub was at least a hundred years old. He must have spent fifty hours cleaning all the paint from those ball-and-claw feet on the bottom. When he finished, we had it powder coated so it would stay pretty."

"It must have worked," the man said. "It still looks brand new."

"Most comfortable tub I've ever sat in. Sam put in a larger water heater so I could fill it up and soak."

"Marie?" the woman called out, walking to the bathroom door. "Marie, where are you?"

"She was on the front porch swing when I came up here," I told her.

Everyone went downstairs, with me bringing up the rear. Marie was still on the swing. Jack lay on her lap, purring. I had left the front door open when I went upstairs.

"What's his name," Marie asked. She had a fluid, almost musical voice with a slight Hispanic accent.

The world was swirling around me from descending the stairs. I collapsed into the chair beside the swing. "Jack." I finally managed. "He's been my companion since my husband died twelve years ago."

Her parents were still staring at Marie in shock. I don't think they would have been more surprised if the Red Sea had parted in front of them.

"Marie, do you like Jack?" I asked into the silence.

She scratched him behind the ears. He arched into the pressure from her hand. "He's my friend," she answered. "If we buy your house, will Jack stay here?"

Her mother reached out to her husband; both had tears in their eyes.

"Could you p-possibly ... part with Jack ... as part of the deal, ma'am?" her father asked, his voice breaking a little when he said the words. "If you could, I promise you; he will get a good home. I think it would mean a lot to Marie and us."

I watched Jack in Marie's lap, then painfully leaned over to them so I could scratch him under his chin. "Jack, is this what you want?"

He closed his eyes and put his head down on Marie's lap.

"OK," I said, looking up. "That was pretty clear. Jack wants to stay."

I studied the couple, imagining them living here, where Sam and I had loved each other for over forty years. Could I turn over this house, our home, to these strangers? My emotions swept over my self-control like a tsunami. Stepping to the edge of the porch, I reached out to the one person I could count on for guidance when all else failed. *What should I do, Sam? Should I let them replace our dusty old memories with their shiny new ones?*

Sam's hand squeezed my shoulder, and his voice whispered in my ear as clearly as if he were standing next to me. "Our memories will always belong to us, Janice. They are the ones."

I spun around, expecting, *praying,* to see him one more time, but of course, he wasn't there. Instead of Sam, four hopeful faces stared back at me.

The decision became permanent. "I'll leave his vet history on the kitchen table with all the papers about the house. My husband and his brother built it and the barn about forty years ago. We used to have horses in the pastures, but I gave them away after he passed. The barn's still all set up for them. Anything else you want to know about the house or the property?"

Marie's eyes lit up even more when I mentioned the barn and horses. She looked back and forth between her parents with excitement. Her parents were still clutching each other's hands, their eyes fixed on Marie in disbelief, boarding on euphoria.

Her father finally answered. "Nope. I think we need to sign some papers at Stan's office. When could we move in?"

"I'll be leaving tomorrow. The house is available any time after. Everything inside goes with the house, as the advertisement said. Do with it what you want, but Jack is particularly fond of that maple ladder-back chair. Be great if you could put it where the sun can hit the seat."

"We'll make sure it's there," her mother promised, her eyes not leaving Marie with Jack on her lap.

I turned to Marie, finally gaining peace, even a little excitement, from knowing that I'd be with Sam soon and that Jack would have a loving home after I left. "I won't be able to feed or care for Jack after I leave tomorrow. So, I will count on you to take over for me."

Marie stroked Jack's head and smiled. "I will take care of him."

I had the feeling it had been a long time since she had smiled at anything. If Jack could have smiled, his would have been ear-to-ear.

A Call in the Middle of the Night

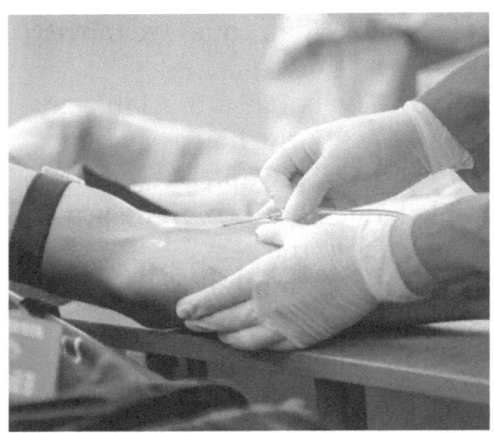

I was sound asleep when the phone rang. The clock next to the bed said 3:32 AM. Cell phones hadn't been invented yet. The phone hung on the kitchen wall of our mobile home.

"Should I answer it?" ran through my head, then I shrugged and walked to the phone.

"Fred, your blood type is O-neg? Right?" I recognized the voice of my wife, a nurse, who was working the graveyard shift at the ER of our local hospital.

"Yep. What's up?"

"We just had a baby born with an Rh incompatibility. It needs a transfusion immediately, and we can't use refrigerated blood. Even with a blood warmer, the doc says fresh blood, right out of a vein, is best."

"I'm on my way." I pulled on my clothes and ran to my car. The hospital was just over a mile away. I'd just finished an EMT course. As I drove there (way too fast), I reviewed what I'd learned about Rh incompatibility in newborns. As I remembered it, when the mother has Rh-negative blood and the fetus growing inside her has inherited Rh-positive from the father, the mother treats the fetus's Rh-positive red blood cells as a foreign substance and makes antibodies against them that cross over to the baby in the placenta and destroy the fetus's red blood cells. When the red blood cells break down, the infant can turn blueish because there aren't enough functioning red blood cells left to carry oxygen around the infant's circulatory system. The metabolized red blood cells may also turn the child yellowish, like jaundice. An Rh reaction only happens in a second or subsequent Rh pregnancy. A first Rh-baby only gets the mother's immune system ready to react to the second one.

"Her prenatal care should have shown this," I muttered. "Why the hell didn't someone check?"

I slid to a stop in a parking spot next to the entrance to the ER and ran inside. A med-tech was waiting for me.

"Mr. Hudgin?"

"Yep."

"We've got everything ready. Please come with me." She handed me a gown, cap, and mask, then walked me to the operating room as I struggled into them. My wife was there, along with the OB doctor and the newborn. The child was under a warming lamp, gasping for breath through its oxygen mask with a blue/gray cast to its skin.

"Sit down, Fred," the doc said. "Thanks for coming. I need your arm. You're O-neg, right? That's what your wife told me."

"Yep." I pulled up the sleeve of my gown and shirt and presented it to him. He started swabbing my inner elbow area with an iodine solution. "Why wasn't this caught in the prenatal exams?"

"She's from Guatemala. Her husband enlisted six months ago to get US citizenship and just brought her up. She hasn't had any prenatal care beyond a local midwife. This is their second child, and no one noticed anything about the first one."

I flinched a little as he stuck the needle into my arm. "How do you transfuse a newborn?" I asked, intrigued.

"Well, a newborn's body only holds a half-pint of blood. So, we put some in and then take some out. It takes a whole pint to replace most of the damaged red blood cells."

"So, the baby is O-pos, and I'm O-neg. Is that OK?"

"It sure is. O-negs can donate to anyone. O-pos can only donate to Rh-pos people."

He hooked my IV line to a syringe attached to a small metal device with a lever on top. A second line went straight into the baby's umbilical cord. He would slowly draw out a syringe of blood from me, flip the lever and push it into the baby. Then he'd slowly draw out a syringe of blood from the baby and pump it into a pan. This went on for ten iterations. With each injection of my blood, the color of the baby gradually went from gray/blue to pink as I watched.

After the tenth pump, he checked the child's vitals and smiled. "Blood oxygen is 98%, her pulse is down, and her color is much better. That should do it. Thanks! You just saved this child's life."

Both the child and I were breathing much easier now. I didn't know how to react to the doctor's praise; that wasn't why I donated blood. So, I smiled, then drove back home (a lot more slowly than my trip *to* the hospital).

.

.

Many years later, I still wonder how the child developed and what kind of person she became. Had I saved a future mass murderer or the person who would discover the cure for pancreatic cancer? Either way, she now had a chance that she didn't have before: to become the person of her future.

With O-neg blood, I am a universal donor (anybody can receive my blood). I have continued to donate, over ten gallons in total now. I began while I was in the army during the Vietnam conflict. The Vietcong Tet offensive of 1968 was in full swing. American casualties were skyrocketing. The army wasn't quite as picky about blood quality then as they are now. All you really needed was a pulse and a drop of your blood sinking into their copper sulfate solution. HIV/AIDS hadn't come along yet. The blood collectors now screen for many diseases before releasing donated blood into the "available" pool.

If you do not donate blood, please think about doing it. There is a huge shortage that grew substantially worse during COVID. You will probably never know who received your blood or if it worked for them. But now, the Red Cross sends me an email when my blood is used. When I get that email, I smile, knowing that somewhere, someone has a chance to continue their life because I took the time to share my blood with them when they needed it most.

Nice Day for a Ride

"All right, get out of here! You've been moping and whining around the backyard all goddamned day. I know you wanna go for a ride. So GO!" My wife turned on her heel and stalked back into the house, slamming the screen door loudly for effect. Josh, Beethoven, and I looked at the door where she had disappeared, then down at the garden where we had hoed, tilled, and planted since breakfast. I looked up at the sky to see where the sun was—still a couple, three hours till dark. A slow smile spread across my face—a ride!

I scratched Beethoven behind the ears. He's not really a St. Bernard, just a big brown dog with floppy ears and cheeks. "Josh, your scooter runnin'?"

"Yep. Blow your antique off the road, Dad," he said, smiling.

"Effin' kids on their Effin' rocket bikes," I muttered to myself as we walked to the barn. "They'll never know how to fix loose timing advance weights with a paperclip." Of course, then, they won't have to, will they? There's nothing mechanical left in their solid-state, fuel-injected ignitions.

I rolled open the door to the barn, and there they were in all their glory: My beautiful, sight-for-sore-eyes, work of art, only a little dented, but none the worse for wear 1981 Harley Sturgis right beside Josh's gaudy, runs-forever-

and-never-breaks, fully-erect, one-year-old, balls-to-the-wall, ported, polished, fuel-injected Harley Evo rocket bike. We both just stood there with these idiot smiles on our faces until another Harley passed by on Route 9, about half a mile away.

In my best Sam Elliot, I announced, "We should be going; daylight's burnin'."

The only thing better than lookin' at Harleys is ridin' 'em. Josh's Evo started on the first touch of his button. Mine would have if I'd remembered to turn on the gas. Really!

We headed out the driveway after the required number of backfires and sputters (mine, not his—I like to think of it as my bike, Moon Dancer, greeting the ride with a breath of fire.) I led until we got to Piedmont and topped off the tanks. There wasn't a cloud in the sky. The temperature hovered just a little over eighty. Both bikes were running great. Where to go, where to go?

Josh was checking out some cuties in a pickup truck getting gas next to us. "How about runnin' up to the dam, Dad?"

"Oh, I don't know," I said, looking around. "All those good lookin' teenage girls just barely covered by their bathing suits. And them beggin' us for a ride around the parking lot. Seems like a lot of bother."

Josh looked at me like I'd lost my mind.

"Oh, all right. Just this once."

Somehow I managed to say that with a straight face. Josh just laughed and touched the start button. His bike roared to life. Moon Dancer only backfired once before she settled into her comfortable chug-aty-chug.

Off we went, the road a blur under our foot pegs, the mighty sound from our exhaust pipes causing every head we passed to turn and smile. This would be a day that memories were made from. An hour later, the sun was inching toward the horizon off to our left as we turned north on the narrow two-lane road that led to the dam, twenty-five miles away. Live oak trees met overhead with glimpses of the beginnings of a beautiful sunset peeking through.

By the time we got to the dam, Venus was fully exposed (the planet, not the woman). Most of the people had already left. There were a few campfires spread around the lake, filling the air with the sweet smell of burning oak. The unmistakable sounds of Lynyrd Skynyrd playin' The Breeze came across the water from the nearest campsite. The firewood sure is aromatic these days, I chuckled to myself. We used to have to spend a lot of money to make smoke that smelled that good. "Ah, youth is wasted on the young," I muttered.

The fireflies had come out, and the bullfrogs and crickets were beginning their nightly duet. The first cool breeze of evening gently passed over us as more and more stars emerged from the dusk. "Well, I guess we waited too long, Josh," I said, turning my bike around. "Everyone's getting' settled in for the night or has already gone home." I could see Josh agreed with me.

He turned his bike around also then pulled up next to me. "Hey, how about stopping at the Wagon Wheel on the way back? I heard they have a kick-ass band this weekend. Dennis told me they did a fifteen-minute Free Bird last night. Said it was like ol' Ronnie VanZant, himself, stood on the stage."

"Sounds good to me," my mouth already waterin' in anticipation of one of the Wagon Wheel's famous cheeseburger gut bombs. "Let's ride." I reached for my leather jacket that should have been tied to my sissy bar and realized it still lay across my toolbox by the door to the barn. "Dammit," I muttered. "Gonna be a cold ride home."

We stopped at the exit to the parking lot as a truck passed by, going the same way we were. It wasn't just any truck. No, from the smell it left hangin' in the air, it was a very special truck. It was hauling hogs.

Now everyone has somethin' they hate more than just about anything else in the world. For me (besides elderly, oriental, male drivers), it is riding behind a fully loaded trailer hauling hogs. Those evil, red-eyed bacon makers feel the same about me. Not only do they have a case of the ass about where they're goin' (hogs being one of the most intelligent animals in the barnyard), they are packed into those trailers until they can't turn around and kick the ass of the poor bastard behind him that's sniffin' their balls. All they can do is stand there, grunt, fart, piss and shit. Since that's all they can do, they do a lot of it. The problem comes when the truck makes a turn, and that wonderful perfume, Essence d'Hog, kind of a toilet water that had been sloshing around their feet, runs out the slots in the sides, down onto the wheels, and is broadcast into the air behind the truck. Anything or anyone behind the truck gets a free application.

Only for me, it's worse. I swear those sons of sows save it up for me until I am behind with no place to go, then they make me pay for every pork chop, slice of ham, and piece of bacon I've ever eaten. You laugh, but it's not funny. You see, it's happened to me enough times that my wife had a hot and cold water faucet installed in the barn for me to hose off before I come into the house. Some guys attract girls. Some guys attract guys. Me, I attract hog trucks. Call it fate.

Josh was just sittin' there on his bike shakin' his head. It's like he can't believe this is happening again. "Dad, you are truly blessed" is all he can manage.

Screw it. The sun is gone, the stars are shinin' in all their glory, the temperature is droppin' like a stone, I don't have a jacket, but I do have a hog truck. Maybe it will keep me warm. Its taillights were disappearing around the next turn as we pulled onto the road.

It's not as bad as I'd feared. Nope, it's worse. The hogs knew they had me. The truck could only go about twenty-five miles an hour down that curvy, hilly road from Hell. Those two yellow lines in the middle of the road slowly burned themselves into the back of my eyeballs. Every so often, I would try to pass only to have to swerve back behind the truck as a car appeared comin' from the other direction. Each time I got close enough to try to pass, the hogs reached deep within themselves to spew yet another geyser of pig offal onto the floor of the truck, which immediately got broadcast into the air I was riding through.

Who would have believed barnyard animals would have enough intelligence to coordinate that kind of team effort? It's like the hogs had a manure gun they all worked together to load, then the fire control officer waited until I pulled within range before he let me have it. "Here he comes! Wait for it. Wait for it. Almost here. OK, everyone, let 'er rip!" You've gotta respect that kind of discipline.

I remember how much trouble I had teaching new grunts ammo conservation in their first firefight. Maybe I should be takin' notes.

My headlight had grown dim from the deepening layer of hog crap building upon its lens when we finally got to the Wagon Wheel. Josh and I parked our bikes well away from everyone else so the smell wouldn't spark some kind of mercy mission from the other riders. The last thing I needed was a bunch of bikers trying to help us out by washing off our bikes using their own private garden hoses.

Josh acted like he didn't want to go in. "Dad, are you sure you want to do this? I mean, we stink! I'm leavin' a footprint trail of hog crap behind me." He had suddenly found something really interesting on the ground next to his bike and was studying it while he waited for me to change my mind.

This is sad, but I gotta admit I was sorely tempted to just get back on my ride and go home. But, hey, this was a biker bar, and everyone knows bikers smell like crap. "Nah. Come on. No one will ever know. These are bikers, fer God's sake."

Well, I was wrong.

I walked in the door, and the music actually stopped. Everyone was lookin' around and testing the air like a bunch of prairie dogs with a coyote on the loose. My favorite waitress walked by and almost dropped her tray full of beers while she gagged for air. "Damn, Crow! You been rollin' in the barnyard again?"

"Sorry, Becky. We got stuck behind another damn hog truck on the way down here from the reservoir."

"Someone up there doesn't like you, Crow. What's this, the third or fourth time this year?" She laughed and walked away ... fast.

I saw some of my friends over in the corner of the bar trying real hard not to notice me. I started over, and suddenly everyone at the table had to go to the can—left at least twenty beers behind in various states of consumption. I heard some bikes start-up in the parking lot, and there went Bedrock by the window in a cloud of dust and dirt followed by the rest of the crew.

I went to the can and thought about whether I should just go home and shower. As I sat on the throne, a guy came through the door and started coughin' and swearin'. "Man, I think you better do a courtesy flush before the paint starts to peel." A couple of more coughs, "Sheee-it that smells bad. Have you ever thought about leaving them burritos alone for a while?" Then he started gaggin' and left without even doing what he'd come in to do.

After I finished up, I came back out. The packed bar I had entered four minutes ago was almost empty. Even the band had gone outside to "take a break". Big Joe came around the end of the bar with a look on his face that would have stopped a charging rhinoceros. "Crow. I know this ain't your fault, but, man, you just gotta leave. If you come in here on a Saturday night again, smellin' like this, I'm tellin' ya, I'm gonna 86 ya.".

About fifty different replies went through my head in that split second. Then I just hung my head and said, "Joe, I'm sorry, man. You're right." And I walked out the door.

The people on the front porch all moved away as I came outside. "Wannabes." I muttered as I walked by.

Josh was still where I'd left him by the bikes, trying hard not to laugh. "That didn't take long. Is there anyone left in there?"

"Yeah." I wasn't in any mood to chit-chat.

"As soon as you went in, it was like you'd kicked an anthill." he went on. "There were bikers kickin', crankin', runnin' and gaggin' everywhere. Funniest thing I ever saw! I almost fell off my bike; I was laughin' so hard."

"Are you ready to go?" I asked.

He could see I wanted to get out of there. "Sure, Dad."

For the first time in her life, Moon Dancer started on the first kick. I believe in my heart she was genuinely embarrassed and couldn't wait to get away from the scent of the crime. We eased out of the parking lot and headed home.

At the first traffic light, we pulled up next to a beat-up family sedan.

I looked over at the old man who was driving and smiled. After a couple of seconds, his head snapped around to stare at me, and he got a look on his face like he couldn't believe what had just drifted up his nose. Just about then, his wife leaned over and let him have it right on the side of his head. "Damn you, Marvin," she shouted. "I told you to lay off them peppers."

"Whatrya talkin' about, ya crazy old bat," he shouted back, then he pointed at me. "It weren't me. It's *him*!" He gave her a dirty look and then gave ME a dirty look and rolled up his window.

They were still sitting there yelling and swinging at each other when the light changed, and we rolled out.

By the time we got home, I had left most of those bad feelings behind me on the road. Josh got out the hose and began to clean the worst of it off the bikes. My wife came out the back door to welcome us home and got halfway across the yard before she stopped dead, then said a little too loudly, "Oh no, not again!" Without another word, she turned on her heel and stalked back into the house.

For just a minute, I considered getting back on the bike and leaving, but where the Hell would I go? The cops were probably already looking for the two crazed bikers that terrorized that old couple at the light. "All right, gimme the damn hose."

Two minutes later, she returned with a bucket of hot soapy water, some rags for the bikes, and towels for us. Together we washed the bikes and ourselves.

"You know," she said. "I kindda knew this was gonna happen. Don't know why, but I knew."

"So, what's for dinner, Mom?" Josh asked as we walked inside wrapped in towels. "Smells great."

She had a Mona Lisa smile on her face. "Somehow, after what happened to you tonight, I think you guys will really enjoy dinner. I've got a big ham in the oven."

Ha

"You wanna Coke? Cold Coke – very cold. Or beer? Have number 1 beer for GI."

"Not today, Ha."

She smiled and moved on to the next truck.

Our convoy had stopped outside of Pleiku. This was normal. The ride up from AnKhe always stretched out over several miles. Those heavy trucks slowed down to three miles per hour, crawling up the steep Mang Yang pass between AnKhe and Pleiku. This was the place where everyone caught up; then we would continue through the town of Pleiku as a group and enter the army base where we off-loaded our trucks. I think the convoy commanders did this as a security thing, so local vehicles couldn't enter the convoy between the trucks as we passed through the town and possibly attack us. The Vietnamese locals had set up an oasis where we stopped, selling anything that would sell—cold cans of pop and beer, souvenirs, trinkets, paintings, sex. The stop was popular with the drivers. We could get out of our hot, noisy trucks, stretch our legs, and get a cold drink after the sweltering, dusty ride.

Ha was a little girl, maybe ten years old, who I enjoyed seeing every time I stopped. She would joke with me in her pigeon-English and thank me profusely when I gave her the unused parts of my C-ration meals that I would save up between trips to Pleiku. She was so skinny and malnourished, a good breeze would have blown her into the next province. Sometimes I bought a cold pop from her just to be able to give her a little cash.

Instead of US greenbacks, our "cash" was MPC (military payment certificates). The GIs had flooded the economy with cash when paid in US currency, buying anything they wanted, primarily whores and drugs. Most of the cash ended up in the hands of the Vietcong. In large part, that's how they funded the war against us. So the powers-that-be now paid us in MPC notes. Every so often, the US forces would collect all the old notes country-wide, and issue us new ones printed in a different style, invalidating the old notes. This removed the value of the money from the Vietcong. When we returned to the US, they converted any of the current MPC notes in our possession into US currency.

    I changed my mind about the cold pop and went in search of Ha. Lots of other Vietnamese kids were working the convoy, just like she did. GIs always have a soft spot for kids of foreign lands. I found her standing next to a truck on the side that was away from all the people and stands. No one else was around. She hadn't seen me yet and was acting strange, almost covert. I slid behind the truck I was next to and watched. She removed the fuel tank cap on the truck and dropped something in. Then put the cap back on, looked around to make sure no one had seen her, and walked quickly around the back of the truck, out of sight.

    I walked to the fuel tank and opened it. Inside was a hand grenade wrapped in what looked like masking tape. The safety pin had been removed. The diesel fuel in the tank would slowly eat through the mucilage on the tape as it sloshed around when the truck went down the road. When the last of it had been dissolved, the grenade would explode, destroying the truck, the driver, and usually the tanker of fuel the truck was pulling.

    I had no idea what to do. I called over one of the gun truck drivers and showed him what I'd found. He called the convoy commander on his radio. The convoy commander, a second lieutenant, listened to my story. I could tell he was pissed off. He told me to find Ha while he called the MPs, then called EOD (Explosive Ordnance Disposal) and evacuated everyone, along with the surrounding trucks, from the area near the truck with the grenade.

    I found Ha hiding inside the little shack where she kept the things she sold. She was crying. "Please no tell, GI! I no do your truck. VC have my family! Kill everyone if I no put in truck."

I was torn. Yeah, she didn't put the grenade in my truck, but she did put it in another guy's. That guy was an American like me. He had family that loved him back home. I figured I had no choice. If I didn't turn her in, she would do it again to someone else. I walked her over to the MPs.

The MPs weren't sure what to do with her either, her being a Vietnamese national. They called the local ARVN (Army of the Republic of Vietnam) MPs. EOD showed up in their bomb suits and pulled the grenade out of the tank. They wrapped it in duct tape and put it in a bomb containment. They left as the ARVN MPs showed up. The ARVNs slapped Ha around and screamed at her in Vietnamese. She tried to talk, but they just slapped her again and again, then put her in handcuffs. I started to intervene, but an American MP put his hand on my chest and shook his head. The ARVNs loaded her into their jeep and drove away. She looked at me over the back of the seat as they left, blood running down the side of her jaw from her split lip.

"What's going to happen to her," I asked the American MP.

He laughed—I'll never forget that laugh. "She'll be dead in a ditch before they get back to their HQ."

I never saw Ha again. I asked the other kids every time we stopped. No one knew. The next time we came through, someone else was using her shack.

Years later, I found out the name "Ha" meant "kiss of life, sunshine, and warmth." I hope she found some of that in her next life.

Who Was Eve Really?

Grock Species Mining Ship GSMS-032 entered real space about half a million kilometers from Earth, the rosy glow of the wormhole portal surrounding its exit like a halo. The ship accelerated into a stable descending orbit to avoid the planet's moon and give them a better view. It appeared to be everything the drone scan had promised.

    Captain Phillium stared at the beautiful world, not believing his luck had finally changed. From what the octopus could see under the intermittent clouds, liquid water covered at least two-thirds of the surface—not the superheated steam and sulfuric acid he had found on the second planet or the mantel, thousands of kilometers thick, of frozen water and methane that covered the gas giants farther from this sun. This one had huge oceans and massive continents with mountains, deserts, and plains, and unless he was wrong, those green areas were filled with forests, rivers, lakes, and grasslands. Life—that's what he was looking at. He pinched himself with his primary tentacle to make sure he wasn't dreaming.

    After nine duds on this expedition, this one had huge potential. Corporate would be thrilled! This was where the big money was: raising-up intelligent life on living planets. No one had mined out this far before. Permission to go somewhere new was hard to get and even harder to get funding for, but all the deals and bribes he had made to middle-level managers were going to pay off—and this star was only the beginning. This tip of the arm of the galaxy contained thousands more systems just like this one, ripe like a basket of perfect fruit waiting for him to claim.

"It's all about return on investment, Captain. You find a Class 1 planet, and we'll invest in you with better equipment."—The frigging accountants ran the galaxy!

The crew knew the drill and went about their jobs enthusiastically. There were so many species onboard, each chosen for their particular talents. Almost every species type in the galaxy had been found on multiple worlds.

With their eight-lobed brains, Octopuses were typically the navigators—perfect for managing both ends of a four-dimensional wormhole jump. Med-techs were primarily arachnids because they could use the front four of their eight legs asynchronously. Felines and heavy-worlders made up Security—felines because they were so ferocious and cunning, heavy-worlders for their massive strength from living in two or more G's most of their lives. Because of their devious nature, primates were most often used in Analysis. Of course, based on individual talents, there were many exceptions. One of the captain's many functions was keeping everyone working together and minimizing inter-species friction.

The crew could see this world had more potential than any claim they had ever found; the bonuses paid to the captain would also trickle down to them. They also looked forward to the "recreational" time while everyone waited for the raise-up virus to incubate. During rec-time, they would have a chance to visit the surface of this beautiful planet and explore the other worlds in this solar system. But they wouldn't get rec-time unless the Galactic Species Control Board (the GSCB) accepted our claim, and the crew had a lot of investigation to complete before they could submit it. The air on GSMS-032 practically crackled with anticipation.

While the company registered their claim, the crew hurried to their stations, preparing to examine the world. There would be plenty of time for play after the work was done.

The technicians released the marker drones as soon as the Drone Control Center was staffed. To begin their scan, the drones descended almost to the surface. Sites where intelligent life might reside had to be examined carefully. Was there any sign of crop cultivation? Had paths or roads been built? Did any population centers exist—villages, towns, cities? If they found technology, how advanced was it?

Each time a likely site was observed, the operators would have their drone release a marker pod—a sphere about ten centimeters across—which would descend the rest of the way to the surface. Each pod had a sophisticated internal AI to guide it, and based on the terrain, the device would configure itself appropriately: on a savannah, its legs could extend up to three meters; in a forest, it could hang from a tree limb; in water, it could float or descend as needed; in a canyon, it could hover; and if a particular configuration didn't work, it could change to a different one that worked better.

Once the pods were in place, they began executing hundreds of tests: atmosphere analysis, soil analysis, water analysis, radio wave detection, radioactive isotope detection, and a hologram high-def photo scan of the surrounding area in fifteen different wavelength ranges. The team gave special attention to identifying and classifying any life forms they encountered.

Several pods had to be replaced soon after they were deployed—two large, furry pachyderms crushed one as they mated, and a colossal grazing herbivore decided another looked good enough to eat.

"Captain to the bridge." The call came through his communicator.

"What's happening?" he asked as he arrived.

"Another starship just arrived. We think it's beginning a species examination."

"Who the hell is it? Are they pirates?"

"I asked. They say they are registered to Quyshargo."

"The Mer-people? What the hell are they doing here? How did they find this system? We're out in the middle of nowhere!"

"They say they found this system months ago and are getting approval to raise-up one of the air-breathing aquatic mammals. They said *we* are claim jumpers and to leave immediately."

Quyshargo was the only world accepted into the Ur with indigenous water-breathing aquatic mammals. The Ur was the loose government of the galaxy's sentient species, controlling all commercial interaction between member worlds. It was no secret that Quyshargo's king mentored aquatic species of all kinds into galactic citizenship, but no one thought they would stoop to piracy to achieve it.

"Open up a commlink to them. I want to talk to the captain."

A floating female Mer-person appeared in the hologram in front of him. A three-inch layer of water surrounded her, supported by the antigrav unit underneath. Her long blonde hair swayed in front of her breasts as the water rippled around her slim, muscular body. They stared at each other without saying anything for a moment.

"You must leave immediately," the being said. "This is our claim." Her voice was almost musical.

"We have registered this claim with the GSCB. It is you who must leave."

"We have also registered this claim. Leave, or we will be forced to remove you."

"Not gonna happen, you overgrown fish egg. Go steal someone else's claim."

The Mer-person's eyes grew hard. "Leave now, or ...."

"They've opened a wormhole!" the exec shouted, hitting the emergency jump button that all navigators kept ready. In space, there were many reasons you would want to be somewhere else within seconds, and every navigator built at least three safe, jump-away coordinates upon arriving anywhere.

The emergency wormhole they had used to escape was still open when the torpedo exploded, and shrapnel peppered the hull of GSMS-032. While most of it had been deflected by the asteroid shields every starship left active while parked in orbit, a few pieces got through, and hull penetration alarms began screaming all over the ship.

"That daughter of a monkrus!" Captain Phillium screamed. "Send a torpedo back at her."

"They've already jumped, sir. I don't know where they are."

"Engineering?" the captain called into his comm unit.

"Yes, sir. Almost done." He paused. "Two penetrations remain unrepaired, sir. One jump coil was damaged. Other than that, nothing vital was hurt. Emergency sealing should be completed within four minutes; permanent repairs will take longer."

"After the breaches are sealed, send me a report of the damages and repair estimates."

The captain turned to Major Ang, his exec, "Twermy, will that jump coil hurt our ability to move?"

"Well, yes, if we jump in a direction that requires using that coil. I'll make sure we don't until it's fixed."

Captain Phillium pondered what to do for several moments. "I want you to move this ship in random directions at random intervals. Do it now—do it often. I don't want to be anywhere more than twenty minutes at a time. Outside of linked-hore communications with the pods, maintain emission silence." Major Ang nodded and began planning his next jump. Phillium pressed his comm button. "Analysis?"

"Yes, sir."

"Find them."

"Yes, sir. Working on it, sir."

He pressed the comm button again. "Communications?"

"Yes, sir."

"Tell Grock Central what's going on—and send them the electronic signature of that Mer-ship."

"Yes, sir."

He pressed the comm button one more time. "Sergeant at arms, report to the bridge."

"Already here, Captain." Lieutenant Yawl Ohmel, a heavy-world primate with four arms weighing over two hundred kilos, stood behind him. After the emergency jump, he'd figured the captain would need him.

"Yawl, wormholes work both ways; if they open another at us, send one of our torpedoes up theirs. Twermy, turn up our shields to emergency power. If Yawl launches a torpedo, jump somewhere else instantly—you don't need my permission. If we launch, you jump. Understand?"

"Yes, sir."

"Do either of you have any other ideas? Beyond waiting for them to send another torpedo, how can we hit them back? I'm not going to let those Mer-people wriggle out of jumping our claim."

Yawl had been working out how to protect the starship since he arrived on the bridge. He answered without hesitation, "I'll send listening posts with linked-hore transmitters into various orbits around the planet. They'll alert us as soon as they detect the fish ship's electronic signature."

Then, an idea occurred to him. "Twerny, can you move us perpendicular to the wormhole exit as soon as we go through—to avoid the blast path?"

"Yes, but things are gonna get broken. This isn't a military cruiser—it's not made for that type of maneuver. They know we have their ship's signature and will assume we sent it to Corporate. Why don't you remind them of that? And where the hell *is* Corporate? Why haven't they dispatched a security detail to protect us?"

"Give me a minute." The captain floated into his secure voice cube on the side of the bridge. Everyone could hear him shouting but not precisely what was being said. Finally, the door opened, and he floated out. They already knew the answer by the look on his face. "All the security teams are busy somewhere else. It looks like we'll have to protect ourselves."

Everyone knew the real reason: they weren't a Class 1 ship at Grock—those ships got the first of everything. But unless the Mer-people took this claim away, they would *become* a Class 1 ship when they left this planet.

Now, the analysis of the life forms became a race against time—billions of huz and all of their bonuses depended on it. The GSCB would award the permit to perform the raise-up to whoever completed their package first. Before they could submit the package, all the data had to be bundled according to the Galactic Species Proliferation Act guidelines.

… … … … … … … … …

The crew became so used to the sound of a jump warning alert that, beyond clasping a jump anchor nearby, most didn't pay any attention to it. The sleeping crew didn't awaken. The eating crew held on to their meals and tightened their containment belts.

The Analysis Center began examining the data as soon as it flowed into the ship's computers from the pods. They ruled out the presence of advanced technology early on—no radio emissions of any kind, no dams on the rivers, no visible roads, no radioisotopes, and no pollution. Some primitive, stick-wielding primates clustered around a water-filled basin on the largest continent about thirty degrees up from the equator and several air-breathing aquatic life forms. Both had intelligence potential.

Grock Corporation had filed a complaint about the Quyshargo ship jumping their claim. The Mer-ship had done the same thing. Data collection pods placed by GSMS-032 kept disappearing or became non-functional. The Mer-ship denied any knowledge of the disappearances and damage, of course, but the Mer-pods began disappearing also. No one had the slightest idea where they had gone. Each time a Grock pod disappeared, the Drone Control Center had to send a new pod down and start its scans over. The result was that data collection was taking far too long for both ships.

Finally, the Grock ship completed its scan. Admin filled out the electronic forms to accompany the collected data and sent the package to the GSCB. The captain got on the shipwide PA system. "The analysis package is being sent. Grock Corporation and I appreciate your hard work in finishing up despite the interference. As a thank-you, I declare a Captain's Holiday even though we haven't yet received approval for our claim.

"Medical has approved visiting the surface; oxygen-breathers desiring it may descend to relax or explore. You must wear your nano sterile suits while away from your lander. I know they feel like you are wearing nothing, but trust them. They will float you to the ground if you fall and protect you against anything this side of a nuke, including biological agents and predators, and still let you feel the wind, waves, and sand.

"Use the waste cabinets in the landers for your bodily functions—we don't want to infect this world any more than we want it to infect you. Always stay in groups of two or more. Bring freeze guns to protect yourselves. And remember to stay away from the possible raise-up species.

"Most important, stay away from the Mer-people's examination areas. Don't let them see you; don't interact with them; if they approach you, return to our ship without delay—don't let them near you. And no souvenirs! We don't know what germs this world has, and we certainly don't want theirs onboard. Other than that, have fun. You've earned it."

The anticipation was over. It was finally here: REC TIME!

Only a combat crew remained on the ship, moving it from spot to spot and securing their claim. The Mer-people's ship was still an unknown, and other pirates could show up at any time.

... ...

The raise-up permit status remained pending—the Quyshargo ship had submitted its application within seconds of the Grock filing, and the GSCB had escalated resolution to the emperor's office. So, there was nothing to do but wait.

The crew had the traditional lottery going as to which species the GSCB would choose for the raise-up, and animated discussions and analyses filled every off-duty place of relaxation. Most crew members chose one of the air-breathing aquatic mammals or the primates, but some thought neither species was ready.

After another three days, the GSCB announced the claim was awarded to Grock Corporation, and the selected species were the primates. They instructed Grock to begin its raise-up.

All the winning tickets from the crew members who'd bet on the primates were put into a box. The captain put on a blindfold and chose one to receive the collected money. It was a popular ceremony that everyone enjoyed. "Six-fifty-nine," he announced into the shipwide PA. Two decks below, a female medical technician squealed in excitement and ran to the bridge. She arrived out of breath and almost stumbled. "Do you have six-fifty-nine, Greeha?"

"Yes, I do, sir. It's right here." The arachnid held out the ticket.

He checked the numbers and announced: "Med-Tech Greeha has won the prize and the right to collect the DNA from this species' Eve. Congratulations, Greeha!"

If her smile had been any bigger, her face would have popped. She had never won a species-picking contest before. She tucked her orange hair behind her green antennae and hoped her mother wouldn't notice how much it needed a trim.

The ship's photographer circled them, making a hologram for the Grock Corporation Community Relations Department.

The captain continued, "As soon as the collection is complete, the DNA from the Eve will be inserted into the SIV-2 for incubation." The SIV-2 was the Species Inoculation Virus. It was the vehicle that delivered the DNA modification to the selected species during the raise-up process. "In a week, we will release the virus and start these primates on their way to galactic citizenship; then, we can move on to the next wonderful world waiting to make us rich!"

A combat team and another medic accompanied Greeha to the surface in case things got out of hand. Primitive animals, especially primates, were sometimes violent and always unpredictable. The team landed near a settlement of the primates and began a careful approach. Greeha, armed with a freeze gun, was in the middle of the team so they could protect her from interference by the other clan members.

While the team was on the ground, the Genetics Lab prepared multiple copies of the SIV-2 virus for the coming DNA; if one virus failed, a backup would succeed. The primates' intelligence would double with vastly increased cognitive powers and brain mass. At least as important, their manual dexterity and use of opposable thumbs would increase by the same amount—intelligence without the ability to make and use tools hardly ever led to an admissible species.

The ground team encountered a group of primates eating in a berry patch near their cave. "Remember to select a female for your Eve," the team commander whispered. "Female primates will have teats on their chests."

She chuckled. "You think a med-tech wouldn't know the difference between a male and female primate?"

He ignored her. "Juveniles are the best candidates, and aim at her chest—it won't hurt her a bit. The Eve will collapse where she is, unconscious. Make sure she's somewhere where she won't be injured by the fall."

Greeha sighted the weapon easily with her front four legs—it was a little heavy for just her front two, which the arachnid used for fine detail work when performing medical procedures. Her other four kept her body stable. The moment before Greeha pulled the trigger, the juvenile female she had targeted turned to look directly at her. Instead of panicking, the female cocked her head and studied the arachnid. She had no fear in her expression, just intense curiosity. Greeha pulled the trigger. The weapon emitted a slight buzz but no recoil. The female primate dropped, unconscious.

The other members of the female's family fled to their cave nearby. Greeha opened the primate's mouth and pressed the DNA collector against her inner cheek. The green light on the side of the collector turned red, indicating a successful collection—a confirmation beep issued from the unit.

"Why do they always call the DNA donor Eve?" Greeha asked the team commander as they returned to the lander.

"Don't know where the term came from," he said gruffly, "but everyone uses it."

"I know where it came from," the backup medic whispered to her from behind.

"Where?" Greeha whispered back, intrigued.

"Eve was supposed to be the first mother of the first species. Legend gives her lots of different names around the galaxy. Eve is the most common."

"That's just an old myth," Greeha laughed, dismissing the whole thing. "Something mothers tell their babies on rainy nights. Nobody knows what really happened."

The old medic shrugged. "Many legends have some basis in fact. Is there really any difference between birthing a new species or being the person whose DNA selects the members to be included—all of them belong because of her."

... ...

Genetics did a cursory scan of the collected DNA and encountered nothing unusual. They saw the necessary changes for the raise-up and quickly built the instructions into the virus. They inserted the Eve's DNA into the SIV-2s and started their incubations. Since many species on a developing planet had a similar genetic makeup, the virus used the DNA from the Eve to identify the exact group of organisms to be modified. Before the SIV-2 accepted any individual for modification, a 99.5% or higher match between the Eve's DNA and the target organism was necessary, ignoring the gender portion of the DNA. Once a candidate passed the identification threshold, the Eve's DNA was discarded, and the rest of the virus took over to perform the actual modifications on the candidate's DNA. This allowed the species' genetic diversity to be preserved, further increasing the chances of the raise-up's success in the long term.

Creating enough virus to disseminate across the surface required five more planet rotations. Even then, only half of the primates would be raised-up—there were just too many isolated colonies of the animals to depend on the virus being carried to the entire population by air or personal contact. All uninfected members of the species would continue on their original genetic path. The raised-up members of their species would eventually overwhelm them—it had happened too consistently for any other outcome to be expected. Modified members would begin to appear within a year as the infected individuals reproduced.

As everyone on the starship waited for the virus to incubate, the captain began to rotate the crew down to the surface. Genetics released the virus to the sergeant at arms after five days of incubation. The distribution vehicle left the ship and traveled halfway to the planet, splitting into sixteen separate modules that descended into the atmosphere. Those sixteen devices flew preassigned patterns as they emptied their reservoirs into the air over the known areas of the primates.

"Captain to the bridge." Phillium rolled his eyes. *What now?*

His exec was waiting for him. "I think the Mer-people just released a raise-up of their own?"

"WHAT?"

"They just sent this on its way to the surface." He pointed to his navigation hologram in front of him, and both of them watched something moving on a trajectory toward the largest ocean.

"Evacuate it into a stable orbit! I don't care what it is—this is our planet now. They can't touch it!"

His exec had expected this reaction; he had readied the evacuation device in anticipation. Moments later, he sent the evacuator via wormhole to intercept whatever the Quyshargo ship had released. The item disappeared from the hologram.

"Send a robot to examine the device in orbit. I don't want anyone near it until we find out what it is."

"Yes, sir. Do you think it was a raise-up?"

"We have to find out before we start screaming foul. If that daughter of a monkrus …."

"Yes, sir." His exec left without hearing the rest of the captain's tirade.

After the robot examined the device and found no explosives, they passed it to Engineering, who disassembled it and gave the payload to Genetics.

The head of Genetics called his communicator an hour later. "Captain?"

"Yes, Palno. What did you find?"

"As you expected, the device was a virus distribution vehicle. It wasn't a raise-up, though; it was an elimination virus."

"Elimination? That doesn't make any sense." A light went on in the captain's head. "They were trying to eliminate the *primates!*"

"No, sir," his exec added hastily. "The DNA doesn't belong to any species below—we crosschecked all of them. Then, as an afterthought, I compared it to the DNA profiles of the species onboard, and ... Captain, the virus was targeted at you—your species, I mean."

"*ME?* Son of a monkrus!" A wave of anger coursed through Captain Phillium. Now, it was *personal!* "How did they get my DNA?"

"It wasn't your DNA, sir—it was from a female—but, as I'm sure you know, any member of your species would have worked, sir. Many starships have an octopus navigator."

The captain still couldn't believe the Mer-captain had done it. She knew he would not allow it to deploy the device—that he would retrieve and examine it. If he had opened the device outside the sterile containment in Genetics, he would have carried the virus back to his home without knowing it. It would have made his race of octopuses sterile and die off over the course of his lifetime. No one had ever found a cure for an elimination virus, and that was the point: why would you have an elimination virus with a cure?

He brought up a real-time hologram of the beautiful blue orb slowly spinning below them. "We will meet again, Mer-monkrus. Somewhere, someday, we will meet again and settle this one-on-one." He made a pirate's rune and spit into his shadow on the deck.

Analysis could detect no trace of them in this solar system—the Quyshargo ship had apparently disappeared into a wormhole as soon as it released the device. So Grock Corporation filed a complaint against the Mer-people. Their king responded, saying he did not know of any species mining ship or species elimination virus.

Before moving on to the next star, the crew had to place the wormhole detectors on the planet's moon and register them with the galactic government via a special initial broadcast. These detectors would do two things: alert the galaxy when this raised-up species opened their first wormhole, assuming they ever did, and protect this world from any other unauthorized intruders while the raised-up primates matured.

Some modified species failed to thrive and disappeared without a trace. However, the few species that did make the cut recouped the expense of all the failed ones. The money to be made from a new galactic member was massive. The mining company got twenty-five percent of all profits from the sale of goods from around the galaxy to the new member and twenty-five percent from the sale of any new technology and products from that member to the rest of the galaxy.

The GSCB acknowledged the registration of the wormhole detectors. Phillium congratulated the crew on a well-done job and alerted them that they were about to jump to the next potential star. When everything was ready, he reached for the jump button and pressed it with one of his tentacles.

... ...

After the rosy glow around the portal from the departing Grock starship faded, a small, non-reflective, non-emitting device, appearing to be an asteroid on the scans, left a low orbit and descended into the atmosphere over the largest ocean. It made its way in a crisscross pattern, leaving a powdery residue in its wake that settled gently on the waves. Then, after its reservoir was empty, it accelerated out of the atmosphere and began its long descending orbit into the oblivion of the nearby star's nuclear holocaust.

This was the first of many genetic nudges for the dolphins. Captain Anemone preferred to use incremental changes instead of the single massive mods that Grock Corporation procedures dictated. Her technique was more expensive and took longer, but the result was far better. The species had a chance to adjust to its newfound intelligence and capabilities without all of the wars Grock's technique seemed to precipitate.

The wormhole she had opened after releasing the elimination device had been a dummy. She hadn't turned on the thrusters to enter it and remained in the same orbit as the Grock vessel on the other side of the planet, and all detectable emissions had ceased while they waited for Grock to leave.

Using conventional propulsion, the Mer-captain began moving her starship toward an intersection with the moon. If she had used a wormhole, the detectors Grock had placed there would report her presence. A week from now, when they arrived on the moon, Engineering would modify those buried detectors to turn themselves off for a one-day window on each rotation of this planet around its sun. This would allow her to return to check on her raised-up species' progress, which no one would ever know. With her little periodic pushes, Captain Anemone had no doubt which species would succeed. She settled into her sleep cell—non-jump travel, even for the small distances around a planetary orbit, took a while.

… … … … … … … …

The first non-detection window for a wormhole departure would begin in just a few moments. The captain's clock's timer gave its alert—the window for a wormhole departure without the detectors sending an alarm was open. She reached out of the water bubble surrounding her and pressed the shipwide jump notification. Seconds later, her starship disappeared into a rosy halo. It was time to get paid.

Fredrick Hudgin

The Chair

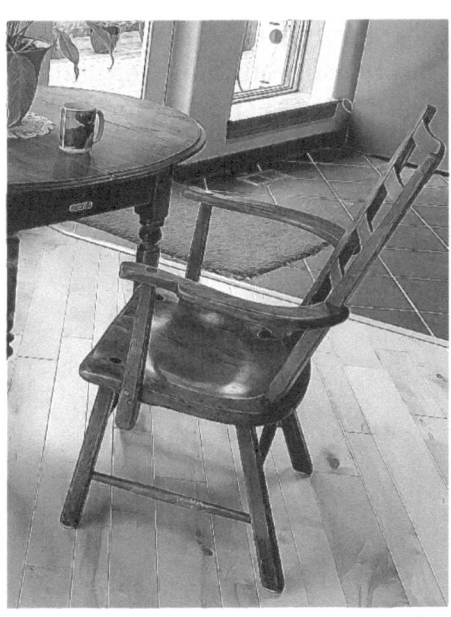

This morning I walked into my living room with a cup of coffee and passed an old chair that was alone in the sun by a window. So, I sat for a few moments and listened to the quiet of the house. Eighty years ago, a carpenter made this chair from maple boards and stained it cherry red. It had faded to a ruddy glow from a lifetime of use. Its sturdy arms and ladder back have withstood the best efforts of three generations of children to rend it, arm and leg.

The girls were at school. My son was off doing errands. I took a sip of coffee, closed my eyes, and let my mind drift to all the memories of which this chair was a part.

I have a picture somewhere of my grandmother holding me right after Mom brought me home from the hospital. She was sitting here with her elbows propped on these solid arms, smiling down at me. I looked up at her with wonder—I did that a lot around Grandma. Years later, when we buried her, I have a picture of Mom sitting here crying.

This sturdy chair has been home to countless feet as we used it as a makeshift stool or as the major support for one side of a blanket fort during Saturday night sleepovers. At least five generations of cats have decided it was a pretty wonderful place to lie in the sun. It's been the extra chair at many Thanksgiving dinners, and Dad always sat here on Christmas morning to hand out presents.

When my first son was born, Grandma and Mom took turns feeding him while they sat here—its arms are the perfect height to support a baby while it takes a bottle. I slept the sleep of the dead, knowing he was safe in their arms.

Now, this chair has come to my house to be friends with the rest of my hand-me-down menagerie. My sister wanted Mom's jewelry. My brother wanted it gone. I had the perfect place for it—right here. Neither Mom nor Grandma will ever again hold a baby in their arms while this chair holds them both.

I feel like I have stolen it—like this chair doesn't belong here since they aren't here to be with it. It should still be in their house instead of mine, and one of them will walk through the door in a moment asking if I need another cup of coffee or help with that baby.

But that won't happen again—at least not in this lifetime. So instead, I will have to hold my children's babies for Mom and Grandma until one of my kids gets to put this chair into their living room and have a quiet cup of coffee while they sit in the sun and listen to their memories.

Coming Home

"Specialist Hudgin, where the hell have you been?"

"Delivering your fuel, Top," I laughed. "Where the hell else would I be?"

First Sergeant Owens was as hard as the diamond in his gold front tooth. Get on his wrong side, and you would suddenly be immersed in a black hurricane beyond your worst nightmare. I'd witnessed his temper a couple of times but had never been on the receiving end.

"Hudgin, you've got twenty-four hours to clear Quy Nhon and get your ass down to Ton Son Nhut Air Force Base in Saigon. Here're your orders." He looked over at our company clerk, Specialist Duncan. "Duncan, carry this sorry excuse for a soldier to finance, to personnel, then to the airport. Get him out of here before I can think of a good reason to keep him in this shit hole for another year."

Duncan walked with me to the arms room, where I turned in my M-16 for the last time, then to the barracks. Packing took five minutes—I'd already sent everything else home. I threw my duffle bag into the back of the jeep, then off we went to collect my records.

On the way into Quy Nhon, we passed a convoy of tankers leaving the tank farm, full of fuel destined for the remote army posts and helicopter LZs (Landing Zones) where the choppers refueled and rearmed. Most of the drivers were from my company, beginning another day in paradise delivering fuel to the American forces in the Republic of Vietnam.

I stood up, hanging onto the side of the jeep, as they passed and waved goodbye. Without exception, they waved back and blew their truck horns. At that moment, I was living the dream every one of them had—to go home to the parents, wives, girlfriends, jobs, and lives all of us had left behind a year ago.

Two hours later, all my records in hand, we were in stopped traffic a quarter of a mile from the entrance to the Quy Nhon Air Base. The air was thick with dust and sounds. Young women and children walked up and down the line of military and civilian vehicles selling anything that would sell—sex, scenes from around Vietnam painted on velvet, fake gold jewelry, Rolex watches that would work until tomorrow, food that had only been dead a couple of days. The smells, as usual, were overpowering: flinty dust, spoiled trash, crap, urine, rancid water, curry, garlic, onions, noodles, and worn-out vehicle exhaust. But mostly dust. Dust covered everything with a light grayish brown—dust that got kicked into the air by everything that moved—vehicles, people, animals, the rare puff of cool air that snuck in from Quy Nhon harbor. Even the rain made dust in Vietnam.

An ancient woman squatted beside us and urinated as we were waiting for anything to move ahead of us. She just lifted her black pajamas pant leg and did her business. She saw me trying to look away and laughed, the lines in her face screwing up like a leather washcloth being wrung out—her one remaining tooth stained black from chewing betel nut.

Men and women passed us on bicycles laden with hundreds of pounds of rice strapped onto the seats, handlebars, and anywhere you could tie a bag. Motorized rickshaws full of produce and animals bound for the market—chickens, fish, hogs. Some dogs looked at me mournfully from their cages as if they knew they would be someone's dinner that night. Small motorcycles with four people on them filled the air with two-cycle pop-pop noise and clouds of blue-gray smoke as they wove through the maze of humanity and animals.

A water buffalo attached to a two-wheeled cart full of handmade chairs was stopped in the middle of the street, being unloaded into a sales stall that was backed up to the chain-link fence around the Air Force Base. The buffalo chewed its cud and looked stoically at us as the traffic slowly parted around both sides of the cart, a pile of buffalo crap on the ground behind it.

The traffic jam disappeared as magically as it had formed, with no reason for it other than too many people going the same way at the same time. The guard at the gate waved us through. At the transportation office, Duncan got out and shook my hand.

We'd never been close during my tour. I'd done a short stint as the company supply sergeant while my truck got repaired. I'd traded in my old manual supply room typewriter for a spiffy new Smith-Corona electric. Duncan had complained to the First Sergeant that I had a better typewriter than he did. The next day, I had Duncan's shitty old manual Remington, and he had my Smith-Corona. I don't think I'd said two words to him after that. And the Depot had said our company was only allowed one electric. Asshole. He could have waited until my truck was fixed.

The flight from Quy Nhon down to Ton Son Nhut took two hours on a noisy, drafty C-123 cargo plane. The pilot stayed at least ten miles out from the coast—so he wouldn't get shot at, I suppose. The seats we sat on folded down from the walls of the airplane and faced the center of the aisle. To see out the window, you had to twist around and look behind how you usually sit. I did that the whole flight, enjoying the panorama of the coast of Vietnam—a beautiful country from 12,000 feet and ten miles offshore—white beaches, dark green palm trees, and blue water.

Behind all of that beauty was the crushing poverty that ground up the people who lived there. I never saw a middle class in Vietnam. There were the few very rich guys, who were in control, and the very poor, who were everybody else.

Ton Son Nhut was even hotter than Quy Nhon. As I waited in line at the out-processing station, a guy behind me from the 4th Infantry Division pulled out a baggy of marijuana cigarettes. I got royally wasted with him and two other guys on that great Nam grass. I told the guy with the joints he'd probably flown in choppers that were burning jet fuel I'd brought to the 4th Infantry Division LZs in An Khe.

He laughed. "Thanks, bro!" and passed me the joint again.

The sergeant in charge of staging us for the next flight to the States had to call my name four times before I realized he was doing it. I just smiled at him and handed over my orders. He laughed when he saw how red my eyes were.

"You board in thirty minutes. Think you can remember that?"

I looked around at the office, then out the windows at the country I wouldn't miss. "I believe I can."

"You wouldn't have any of that left, would you?" he asked conspiratorially, in almost a whisper, while he raised his eyebrows hopefully.

I laughed at that. "Nope. Figured I should finish before we boarded."

"Damn."

Thirty minutes later, I was standing on the tarmac, waiting my turn to board a big, silver Boeing 707 with Flying Tiger Airlines painted on the side. One jet engine was running on the other side of the plane. The scream from that engine made all other sounds fade to insignificance.

The heat rose from the concrete, making the hills behind the base vague and indistinct. It had to be 130 degrees there, standing in the sun. A couple of guys got wobbly and sat on the ground, but no one passed out. No one was going to lose his chance to get on the Freedom Bird for his ride back to the normal world.

The door opened, and the second American woman I'd seen in a year stood at the top of the stairs beckoning us to board. She was short, slim, and Italian-looking with shoulder-length black hair. I blinked for a second, unsure if she was real or just an illusion from the pot; then, we started shuffling aboard.

The other American woman I'd seen had been in the Red Cross Happy Hooch in Quy Nhon. She'd given me cold Cokes and a smile both times I'd been able to visit. She was black, plump, and laughed a lot. Her hair made a soft ball around her head. I hope there's a special place in Heaven for her.

The senior officers and senior enlisted men got to sit up front in first class. The flight attendants seated the rest of us from the back of the plane up to where first class began, every seat filled with a healthy, muscled young man, eager to return to his memory of a normal life. I got a window seat. Through the window, I watched our duffle bags being loaded into the belly of the plane. Half an hour later, the plane began taxiing to the runway's end.

The runway at Ton Son Nhut is two miles long. We had to wait for a pair of F-4 Phantom fighters, bristling with rockets and bombs, to launch, then our pilot began his roll. We went faster and faster, then lifted off the concrete, and I felt the landing gear retract. We were still only ten feet off the ground and about halfway down the two miles of concrete.

I thought about that. The hotter the air, the faster the plane has to go to get enough lift to take off. Add the weight of the men, fuel, and baggage, and I began to worry. Maybe we were too heavy to gain altitude. It would be just my luck to die in a plane wreck while I was *leaving* Vietnam. We kept going faster and faster until we got to the end of the two miles. The pilot pulled back on the stick, hard. It felt like we were going vertical.

He got on the intercom after we leveled out at 10,000 feet and explained that he did that to discourage any snipers from taking one last shot at us. I appreciated that. I'd been through too much hell to get shot as I was going home.

The only times you worried about dying when you are in-country were the first and last months. When you first got there, everything was scary, and you were sure you would die. Then you settled down, learned your job, and got so busy you didn't have time to worry about anything else. When you finally got to your last month, you started to worry that you wouldn't make it to the end.

The trip from Ton Son Nhut to McChord Air Force Base, next to Fort Lewis, Washington, took twenty-four hours. We landed at Midway Island in the middle of the night to refuel. I slept most of the way like everyone else, then woke as we were descending through the clouds above Seattle.

The plane went through one layer of clouds after another with no ground in sight. Suddenly we broke through a cloud layer—the setting sun behind us, lighting up the clouds above and below us with shades of sunlight that went from almost grey to brilliant, burnished gold. It was like my future life was welcoming me back. I started to wake the guy next to me so he could see it also but decided against it. There wasn't time. No one else witnessed our welcome but the pilots and me. I don't think I breathed for those ten seconds. Then we were into the next cloud layer, and the sun disappeared.

Fifteen minutes later, we touched down at McChord and rolled to a stop. The plane was silent. Outside, the lights of McChord Air Force Base were visible through the light rain. No one could believe we were back in the US—that for us, the war was over. Then simultaneously, every soldier onboard erupted into a spontaneous, wild-assed cheer. We'd made it back alive!

At Fort Lewis, we went through classes about what we could and couldn't do when we were turned loose. No defacing the uniform. No embarrassing the government. We were still in the army for 24 hours after we signed our discharge papers, and we could be prosecuted if we did anything stupid. Our government was proud of us and our service ... I slept through most of that too.

A doctor gave us a short physical to see if we had any diseases they wouldn't let into the US of A. When he finished, all of us turned in our faded jungle fatigues and got a new summer weight Class A uniform with black shoes to wear home.

The summer-weight Class A uniform is a lightweight, cotton-wool, grey-green suit with shiny brass buttons and a foldable overseas hat that matched the color of the uniform. Our rank insignia and unit patches were sewn onto the sleeves. The two Vietnam Service Ribbons were now next to the National Defense Service Ribbon I'd been awarded after Basic Training. I felt a moment of pride when I put my Expert Marksmanship badge under the ribbons.

After three years, I could still remember the elation I'd felt when that last target had fallen on the rifle range, and I'd qualified expert. My dad had won the same badge when he'd been in the army. Two combat service bars were now on the sleeve, one for every six months in a combat zone.

Twenty-three hours after I landed in Washington State, I was standing in front of a rosy-cheeked, blond second lieutenant with his one National Defense Ribbon proudly displayed above his Basic Marksmanship badge. I bet to myself that he only had to shave once a week—he looked younger than me, for God's sake.

"Do you understand that when you sign this DD-214, you will no longer be in the army? These are your discharge papers."

I couldn't believe that he had asked me such a stupid question. "Gee, I dunno, can I ask my wife?"

He looked out the window, shook his head, sighed, then handed me the pen. I wonder if he wrote down the things GI's said when he asked that—got to be a book there.

I picked up the pen and realized, at that moment, I was the shortest guy in the army. Shortest means I had less time remaining on active duty than any of the two million or so GI's still serving. As people counted down their days, they got to the last ninety and started screaming "Short!" Invariably there would be a shouting contest as to who *was* the shortest within earshot. "Shorter!" was always the reply when "Short" was screamed. Then people would start announcing how many days remained. "Twenty!" "Eleven!" "Three!" "Tomorrow!"

I turned to the guy behind me in line and said, "Short," so quietly only he could hear. He started laughing but didn't say a word. He understood exactly what I was saying. I signed the two copies of my DD-214s. The lieutenant signed them and handed me back one to keep.

"Protect this," he told me. "It's an important document. Anywhere you want to work will want to make a copy. You'll also need it if you decide you want to reenlist or claim any veteran's benefits."

At that moment, reenlisting was *not* at the top of the list of things I wanted to do. I walked over to the queue waiting for transportation to the airport.

An hour later, I got off a big olive-drab bus at Sea-Tac airport with sixty other men in summer weight greens. White, black, yellow, and brown people were everywhere, speaking English, French, Chinese, Korean, Spanish, and Japanese. They were going in different directions, waiting for tickets, waiting to board, waiting for taxis, waiting for loved ones to arrive.

I just stood there without any idea of what to do while people pushed around and past me. Babies were crying; teenagers looked around as they followed their parents; and men and women shoved their way through the crowds. I wouldn't have been surprised to hear Rod Sterling's voice fade in from the background. "You have just entered the Twilight Zone."

I blinked, then laughed out loud. I was back!

After I got my ticket, I made my way to the gate, where I had to wait until 5 P.M. to board a United Airlines 747 bound for JFK Airport in New York City. The sun was just setting again as we took off through the clouds above Seattle. I looked out through the rain, but that special welcome home from the setting sun I'd gotten on the flight into McChord was not to be repeated. I put my seat back and tried to go to sleep.

A few minutes later, I felt a hand on my shoulder. A flight attendant was leaning over me. "Did you just come home from Vietnam?"

"Yes, I did," I said, smiling up at her. She was a little older than me, but she was cute and smiling at me.

"Come with me," she said quietly.

I got up and followed her toward the front of the plane, wondering what would happen next. We went into first class. She indicated an empty seat.

"You can sleep up here. These seats are a lot more comfortable."

I looked back and forth between her and the seat. "Really?"

"Yep. My brother's still over there. Enjoy the ride. Would you like something to drink?"

"Sure." I reached for my wallet. "Scotch, rocks."

She laughed. "Put away your wallet. The drinks are free up here. Thanks for your service."

The guy next to me was already asleep and snoring quietly. I had two drinks, then slept like a baby for the rest of the way across the country. I guess my body was still catching up on missed sleep. There's always something more important to do than sleep in a combat zone.

I awoke as we rolled up to the gate at JFK. It was January 17th, 1971, 7 A.M. The captain announced the temperature outside was 17 degrees. He said it like it was a private joke. The summer weight uniform I wore didn't seem nearly as warm as it had in Seattle. Another GI I had been discharged with talked his parents into giving me a ride to his home in Elizabeth, New Jersey.

His whole Polish family had come to welcome him home. His six-year-old sister had to sit on my lap for the hour-long ride from JFK to Elizabeth. Finally, she put her head down on my shoulder and went to sleep as we crossed the Verrazano Narrows Bridge to Staten Island. Through the car window, I looked across New York harbor at the Statue of Liberty and the southern tip of Manhattan. The twin towers of the World Trade Center stood tall and proud.

They dropped me off at the side of the road on Route 1. His sister waved at me through the back window as they drove away, her face framed by her beautiful blonde hair.

I'd decided not to call my parents to tell them I'd been discharged until I'd gotten to Sea-Tac. They'd been crushed. Both of them were in all-day meetings today and couldn't come to pick me up. So I picked up my duffle bag, walked to a likely spot, then stuck out my thumb.

I'd heard all the stories about soldiers getting called baby killers when they came home, having rocks and worse thrown at them. Now here I stood on the side of the road in my new uniform, asking for a helping hand to get home.

Week-old snow and ice, now a dirty gray, lined the roadside. Tractor-trailers and cars roared by, pelting me with cold air, salt dust, and diesel fumes. Two blurry days ago, I'd been standing on the tarmac at Ton Son Nhut in 130 degrees.

I figured I had about half an hour before I'd have to go find someplace to warm up. One car after another passed me by. Sometimes the kids in the back seat would wave. I waved back, then put my hands in my pockets. Surely someone would give me a lift; someone would remember a lowly truck driver soldier didn't make national policy.

A police cruiser in the fast lane saw me, turned on its red lights, and pulled over to stop just past where I was standing, barely missing a Camaro and a station wagon that swerved out of his way. He talked on his radio for a minute, then got out and walked toward me.

This wasn't going to be good. I'd only been back in the US for two days, and already I'm in trouble with the cops. Shit. They could have waited until I'd gotten home. At least the jail would be warm.

"Did you just get home from Vietnam?"

"Yep. 359th Transportation Company, Quy Nhon."

"Get in." I started to get in the back, wondering how Dad would react to me calling him to make my bail. "No, not the back," he laughed. "Get in the front." So I did, wondering what would happen next. "Where are you going?"

"Princeton Junction."

"I can only take you to the Elizabeth city limits," he apologized, "but I've already called ahead to Piscataway. They're going to meet us there."

Sure enough, when he pulled over, another police cruiser was waiting with its lights on. Piscataway took me to the city limits of New Brunswick. New Brunswick took me to East Brunswick. Cop cars sure look a lot different in the front seat than they do from the back.

Each of the cops told me about his tour in Vietnam, Korea, or World War II. Each one thanked me for going. Each one called the next jurisdiction to set up my next ride and shook my hand when I got out. I leap-frogged down Route 1, an honored guest of cops instead of a perpetrator, on my way to jail.

"East Brunswick said they had a traffic call and would be about five minutes. Will you be OK?"

"Sure. Thanks for the ride."

"No, buddy. Thank you." He shook my hand. I got out, and he drove away.

As long as I was waiting anyway, I figured I might as well see if I could get a ride, so I stuck out my thumb. A ratty old pickup immediately pulled over. "Throw your bag in the back," the driver called out.

I did, then got in. He pulled his tool belt to the middle of the seat to make room for me. He was wiry and sixtyish with short gray hair, dressed in layers of construction clothes with a week growth of salt and pepper whiskers growing out of his creased, leathery face. His calloused hands and neatly patched clothes were stained with dirt and paint.

"You just get back?"

"Yep. Going home to Princeton Junction. My folks couldn't pick me up."

We rode in silence for a while. "You see some shit?" he finally asked me.

"Nothing really bad. I drove a truck, a 5,000-gallon tanker of fuel. We resupplied the bases and LZs up and down the coast from Quy Nhon, in the middle of the country. Now and then, we'd go to An Khe and Pleiku in the central highlands."

"A tanker of fuel in a combat zone? I think you saw some shit. Tell me how to get to your parents' house."

We rode along in his old truck, him spitting in a cup, me watching ordinary people living ordinary lives. This is why I went to Vietnam, I told myself, protecting these people who didn't even know I was there.

Half an hour later, we pulled up in front of my parents' house. It looked like a Christmas card—the lights and wreaths still up and snow in the yard. I started to get out.

The old man put his hand on my arm to stop me for a second. "Thanks for going. I know it was hard, but thanks. I did my tour in the Pacific during WW II. First Marine Division. From the beginning to the end." He reached down and knocked on his leg, which gave a hollow *thunk*. "Got this in Okinawa."

I didn't know what to say. I loved studying the history of war. Those Marines in World War Two had defined what "saw some shit" meant. He'd fought through the bloodbaths of Guadalcanal, Peleliu, and Okinawa. The First Division had slugged it out with the Japanese for almost four years, hopping from island to island across the Pacific. They'd suffered through 139% casualties. Twenty-two Division members received the Congressional Medal of Honor, most posthumously. All I'd done was drive a truck for a year.

I thanked him for the ride, swallowed hard, and got my duffel out of the back. He got out too, walked around his truck with a distinct limp, and shook my hand. Without another word, he got back in.

While he drove away, I stood at attention and gave him the last salute of my Army career, proud that I could do it while I was still in uniform.

The Beer Drinkers Guide to the Universes

I introduced Mirdu, my new girlfriend, to my friends: Jacam, Griffelda, and Ku, at The School of the Gods, where we were all students. She was a little intimidated by them. Mirdu and I were the only primates in the group. Jacam was a muscular, sky-blue water buffalo, weighing over 2,500 pounds, with golden eyes around his head, and a tuft of blue feathers coming out between his ears. Around his neck and descending his back in bands was a collar of contrasting orange, black, and white feathers. Griffelda was a lion-sized griffin with eagle wings, claws, and teeth. Ku was an energy being who appeared as a ball of light when he wasn't in his crow form. He fed directly from the sun.

"You guys are like legends here at the school," Mirdu said reverently.

"Wait till you smell one of Jacam's legendary farts!" Griffelda said with mock seriousness.

Jacam held out a claw to Griffelda. "Help me out, here," he begged.

"Not on your life!" She put on a terrified expression, then cracked up. "I still have scarring from the last one."

Mirdu became one of our circle and was treated like she'd always been there. We visited each other's worlds, except for Ku's. His didn't exist any longer, having been blown up by a world war. Instead, he found a similar world, and we visited it.

We got to experience what the bodies of that world felt like, changing into those forms as we entered the world. The feathers of Jacam's species tickled my back until I got used to them. A cute, young female water buffalo became seriously interested in Ku and followed him all over. I didn't know anything about how energy beings mated, but I suspected it was nothing like Jacam's species. Ku was a little confused about what was going on until I clued him in. He actually blushed, then tried to explain to the young female that we were aliens in her world. She left in a huff, thinking he wasn't interested in her.

We got to experience the thrill of a sunrise on Ku's energy world. That world had no predators, no plants beyond fungi, and sulfur-smelling geysers that supplied water to everything. His race fed directly from the sun and was *nothing* like I expected. It was as close as I've ever felt to what a female orgasm must be like. As the sun came up, my almost sexual excitement built and built, then exploded into a million stars of light that went on and on. No one ever wondered again why he was always so excited about breakfast.

On Griffelda's world of griffins, I got to fly. The closest I'd ever been to flying before was in a sailplane. And sailplaning wasn't anything like flying with your own wings. The feeling of freedom was incredible, a thousand times better than I'd hoped. You could feel each wind current. You were one with the air.

I used to lay on a hillside when I was a kid and watch the hawks float on the thermals, dreaming of doing the same thing. Ku had no problem with flying at all. He had been flying in his crow form since he was born.

Griffelda showed Mirdu, Jacam, and me how to do some basic aerial acrobatics. Then a male griffin approached our group while Griffelda showed us how to do a chandelle, a climbing bank turn that faced you back the way you'd come. He did a swooping flyby followed by a loop, a roll, and a tailslide, passing us inverted.

She ignored him until he came out of the sun and screamed past us, barely missing Griffelda with his talons. He must have been going a hundred miles an hour. The race was on! Griffelda ported up above him, then dropped like a stone. He saw her coming, banked into a tight spiral, and was on her tail as she passed. They pulled out inches above the huge meadow beneath us, flying so near the grass and wildflowers that some of the blossoms were knocked off.

The male was so close behind her his beak was almost touching her tail feathers. They looked like one being from our altitude. Griffelda pulled up at the edge of the meadow, her feathers brushing the leaves on the trees. The male didn't react in time and hit a tree limb, then spun out of control, disappearing into the forest. Griffelda did a wingover and followed him into the same place. By the time we got there, she was holding him.

"Jeremiah, help me!" she cried out. "He's hurt bad, and I've never done a healing."

Mirdu reached her first. "Put your hands over his wounds and reach within yourself, thinking him whole and healed."

She did. His wounds closed.

"He isn't breathing!" Griffelda cried out in dismay. "What did I do wrong?"

"You didn't do anything wrong, Griffelda. It's a two-step process. Now that his wounds are healed, pick him up and breathe life into him."

Griffelda picked up his head, sealed his nose, and blew into his mouth. Nothing happened. She did it again and again in desperation. Suddenly she realized the male was breathing, had been for a while, and was kissing her back.

She dropped him to the ground with a growl of frustration and turned her back on him.

"Now *that* was a flight to remember!" The male laughed as he got to his feet and stretched. "I liked that last part the best!"

He stared at his wing in disbelief. It had been horribly broken when he crashed. He extended it with a curious expression on his face. "How did you do that? How did you fix my wing?"

Griffelda roared and launched herself up through the break in the trees the male had fallen through. He followed her.

The four of us watched them frolic in the sky together until they disappeared behind a nearby mountain.

We practiced the maneuvers Griffelda had shown us and some Ku came up with until Griffelda showed up a couple of hours later. The male had disappeared.

When we visited my world, we changed into primates using images from inside my head. Jacam became a huge black man with sunglasses, a shirt with Bob Marley's visage on the front, a green, yellow, and black knit beret over his dreadlocks, raggedy shorts, and sandals. Griffelda looked yummy in a black leather vest joined in the front with chains and snaps, like bikers wear, black leather pants, and thick-soled motorcycle boots. Ku was wearing an athletic warm-up suit with the Olympic logo, the South Korean flag above it, and Nike cross-trainers on his feet.

After we finished exploring each of our worlds, we were sitting on a patio in a bar back at Heaven in the early evening. Some god had a full-sky demo of the aurora borealis going on. In a moment of (beer-induced) clarity, I realized that, as different as the worlds were, one common thread existed between them. You might wonder what it was—Compassion? Good people? Bad people? Violence? Peace?

Those worlds had all of those things to a greater or lesser degree, but that wasn't the common thread. What was it, you ask? It was yeast. Yeast is one of the simplest plants ever to be created. Every world we visited had yeast, and in every one of those worlds, we found beer in one form or another. It never ceased to amaze me how many things could be used to make a foamy, frosty glass of beer, from the lightest pale ale to the darkest chocolate stout. Ku told us his energy world had a mushroom beer. Depending on which mushrooms were used, that beer could get pretty exciting.

We made a point of trying as many different local beers as we could each time we entered a new world. We decided to create a Beer Drinkers Guide to the Universes so future classes could build and expand upon it. We spent a week of evenings remembering and creating descriptions and critiques of each beer we'd sampled. Universe, world, country, city, bar, beer. We attempted to rate them as a group, but our preferences interfered with that. So, we ended up having a section for each member to do an individual rating and built a composite rating based on the summation of the individual ones. We also included a rating of the bars that served the beers. Other members of our class heard about what we were doing and wanted to become part of the canvass teams. We visited their worlds, and they visited ours.

Mirdu had a technique for learning the indigenous languages in each world. "People are open books until they learn how to block. It just takes a few seconds of picking their brains, and then you can speak their language as they do."

That turned out to be invaluable. The translator that we had installed into us on the first day of school let us understand whoever was talking to us, but the people in the worlds we visited couldn't understand *us*. So, instead, we became walking, talking, breathing members of each world's species when we went there. We got closest to being discovered on Earth. A couple of rednecks in Mobile, Alabama, decided we "weren't from around here," and they were "gonna kick our asses." Griffelda was in her superhot, Nordic biker chick humanoid form. She grabbed both of them by the crotch and lifted them so their toes barely touched the floor. Then she walked them to the door, with them walking backward and trying really hard not to fall over something. She let her eyes glow slightly red to make sure they understood it was time to go. They got the message. We heard the sound of their old pickup truck leaving rubber in three gears as it left the parking lot.

Out of the hundreds of worlds and thousands of bars and beers we tried, my absolute favorite was a beer and bar on Jacam's world—a little microbrewery bar with a name no human could pronounce on a lake surrounded by snowcapped mountains. The beer name was something like grunt-squeak-blat. The only thing I wanted to do when I finished one was get another. You could rent a sailboat at the bar to sail out on the lake, and the boat came with a cooler full of that wonderful beer. I would go out in the morning and sail all day. I never finished sailing across the lake — it was enormous. And Jacam's species didn't get sunburned! I would float along, enjoying the wind, water, and great beer until the beer was gone. When the beer ran out, I would return to the bar and get some more. There weren't any water cops. No one cared if I was drunk. The only boats on the lake were wind or muscle-powered. I still return there when I need a quiet place to think and relax.

The Mission

It's snowing. Man, this is perfect. Well, I'm still going. After forty-three years of missing Daytona, hearing about how great it was, about all the pretty girls and great parties and dynamite bikes, I'm going. And I'm gonna ride my bike. She may not win any of the bike beauty contests while I'm down there, but she will get me there and get me back. And only break down a couple of times.

I've been packed for a week. I laid an extra coat of wax on everything you can put wax on, tied on all my gear, and just left her chained up in the middle of the garage. The tank's full, everything's tightened and adjusted, and the fluids are all new. I even put on new sprockets and a chain—that tall ratio will be great when we get up on the highway and start cruising. ... Cruisin' in the *snow*. Man, I wish it would slow down a little.

I wonder how far south you have to go before the snow stops. It's about two hundred miles to the Kentucky border. Maybe chains would work on a bike. Goddammit, winter is almost over! What the hell is a snowstorm doing in Indiana at the end of February? This is just perfect.

My wife is so pissed off at me for going on this 'wild goose chase' and 'pretending you're a kid again' that she went to stay with a girlfriend until I'm gone. My kids managed to tear themselves away from the TV long enough to hug me and ask for a T-shirt. All the other creeps I drink and work with said, "Yeah, man, count me in. I'm goin' for sure." They're all snuggled down in their warm little hidey-holes like groundhogs. "The weather's gonna be lousy, man." "I went last year. I can skip a year." "I'm a little short on funds right now." Every one of them. It was gonna be great. Well, I'm still going.

Six inches and still fallin' like gangbusters. My boss gave me a hard time from the moment I told him I wanted the time off. "We're way backlogged, man. Can't you go next year?" "I'll give you a little extra if you stick around." "Aren't you a little old for this?"

I'll be too old when I'm dead. I'm going!

When it gets to nine inches, we go to plan B. I know some guys say "If you don't ride all the way, you're a wannabe, washout, armchair biker, blah, blah, blah." They don't live in Indiana in February. Plan B is my pickup. They don't make them like that anymore. Thank God. I think the rust is the only thing that's holding it together. Twenty-seven years ago, Dodge Motor Company built this truck for the Navy. It lived in salt air and salt winters for twenty years in Rhode Island. I bought it from the Navy when they thought it was worn out. We have gone places and seen things those poor sailors on the Navy base only dream about.

One time we were all drunk over at Bungie's. It was about two-thirty in the morning when suddenly Shelia and Patty had this great idea to play strip poker, but instead of using cards, everyone took off their clothes one piece at a time. The last person with clothes on wins.

So there we were in various states of undress when who walked in but our newest city cop. He had seen the lights on after closing hour and wanted to check it out. This guy *had* to be all of *eighteen* years old. He just stood in the door with all of his cop stuff on, looking at us like he couldn't believe what his eyes were seeing. Finally, Shelia went up to him and invited him to the party. His eyes never got above her navel as he said to keep it down and don't drive home drunk. Good advice. I ended up sleeping in the cab of my worn-out truck with Shelia tucked in next to me. Indiana winters may be miserable, but Indiana summers make up for it.

It looks like it's plan B. All right, I don't care. I'm still going. Put the bike up in the back, stash all my gear inside, a couple of cases of beer ("for when I stop, officer"), tools, and money. I'm ready. I'm *really* ready. Screw all you guys. I hope it snows the *whole time I'm gone*. Snow up to your *armpits*. While you are shoveling this cold, white, fluffy stuff, I'm going to be laying on the beach getting sunburned and drunk while I watch the world's prettiest eighteen-year-olds vie for the title of 'Miss I-Have-The-Smallest-Swim-Suit.'

The truck won't start. Dammit, it's not *that cold*. OK, breath deep. Say "Ooooooom." It worked for Cheech; give it a chance. Once more, slowly. Truck, this is your last chance. Start now, or I swear to God I'll bury you whenever the ground thaws out enough to dig a hole. Come on, baby; you can do it. Once more for daddyyyyy. Wow! It worked. You just got to be tough with 'em once in a while.

Interstate 65 South. Plug in the iPhone (who would have believed this old truck could sound this good?). ZZ Top channel on Pandora, then BB King, then who knows. I've driven through Kentucky, Tennessee, and Georgia before. To call the music selection off the air abysmal is being kind. Hey, I like Hank Williams and David Allen Coe, and if that were what they played, I'd have no problem with it. But no one wants to play that stuff anymore. I guess they got bored listening to good music, so they made up some screechy, whiny stuff and got some guy who looks like he lost a fight with a blender to sing it—can't hold a candle to Ted Nugent or Molly Hatchet at warp volume.

I hope my room looks out over the beach. What a concept! Going on a motorcycle run that lasts a whole week and getting a hot shower and a bed every night instead of a cold stream and a sleeping bag. I want to put my feet up on the railing and watch the sun come up as I smoke the day's last cigarette, then go to sleep. The *only* time to see dawn is from the dark side.

Louisville. Cold iron bridges. Cold stray dogs. Cold concrete roads. Potholes so big, they have teeth on 'em. Snap at ya as you drive by—no passive potholes in Louisville. I heard every Spring they find a couple of bikers in the bottom with their hand still frozen to their throttle and a fixed scream on their face. Ugly way to go: being a landfill for a Mazda. Hard to believe in two months, it will be warm, green, and flowered, just in time for the Derby. Maybe there's a lesson there. Today it's just another gray, dirty town in winter. At least the snow stopped.

Maybe this will turn out all right after all. If I were riding my bike, I would be playing the same music in my head. God, there's nothing like Lynyrd Skynyrd at night on a country road with the moon so bright it looks like daytime. You weave in and out of the tree shadows, and on long straightaways, you can turn off your headlight and still see perfectly. Watch out for turns under the trees, though. There's blood on *that* lesson.

I-285 going around Atlanta. Man! Some poor scooter tramp is out there hitchhiking. What the hell—no one deserves to do that. It couldn't be more than twenty degrees outside.

"Hop in, buddy. Who'd have believed it'd be this cold in Atlanta. Where you going? No kiddin', me too. Too bad about your bike. You'll get her up when you get back. Sure, I'll have a brew."

The miles sure go faster when there's someone to talk to. It may not be Spring yet, but it's a lot warmer than Indiana, and it's not *snowing*.

Goin' through South Georgia always makes me nervous. I have this image of a fat-bellied state trooper with mirrored sunglasses that keeps popping up in my mind. Being the next Cool Hand Luke is *not* on my top 10 list of

"What I Want to Be When I Grow Up". Well, we'll just do the speed limit and ease down the road.

A roadblock! I *knew* we shouldn't have gotten off the interstate. Why did I let him talk me into it? And, of course, that guy is signaling *me* over. I don't believe it! Everybody was passing *me*! And we're In *Georgia,* of all places. I know, I know. Everyone else didn't have a Harley in the back of their truck. I should have known. Hell, I *did* know. Damn. Damn. Double damn. Things were just going too well.

There he is in person. The nightmare *lives*! Jackie Gleason himself. They must go to school to learn how to look like that. He's even *smiling* as he walks up to my truck. Wait a minute. My *hitchhiker* is smiling back. Why do I smell a rat? "Hi, *Uncle* Joe." "We've got *another* one!" I got one last look at my life savings sittin' in the back of my truck before they closed the van door.

The rest of the night was a blur of in-processing to the county jail. "You got any drugs, boy?" "You belong to a gang, boy?" "You got a license for that gun, boy?" "Bend over real far. This won't take a minute." When I finally got to lie down under some stinking moth-ball blankets, I could hear them drag racing my bike against the hitchhiker's rice rocket. Eventually, one of 'em lost it, and they both went down hard. I knew my bike wouldn't put up with that shit very long. From the number of paramedics that showed up in the courtyard, she hurt 'em both really bad.

"Hey, wake up."

I looked up into the face of our club president. Suddenly I was wide awake. "Did they get you, too, Joe?"

He looked at me weird. "Come on, man, everyone's outside. We're ready to go. Big storm's comin', and we have to beat feet."

I sat on my bike while it warmed up. Everyone was stretchin' and tuckin' and zippin'. Finally, I looked over at Joe. "No hitchhikers, man. Promise me no one stops for hitchhikers."

The Second Chance

The inside of the bar was smoky. No one seemed to notice as I sat down and ordered some Jack Daniel's. "Straight up, Joe."

"Sure thing, Wild Bill." he grinned as he poured two fingers of amber liquid into a glass, took my money, and walked back down to the cute redhead he had been talking to.

God, that tasted good. I looked around more slowly this time. There were a few regulars, a couple of bikers playing pool, and one drunk blonde crying in the corner. Pretty normal. I flagged Joe back over.

"Joe, hit me again." That one followed the first, and I was working hard on the third when Lynn came through the door.

"Hey, Bill. Whatcha been up to?" He threw his leg over the stool.

I studied the bottom of my glass for a moment. "Nothin' much," my voice as low as my mood.

Lynn looked at me carefully. "I saw you leaving town this morning like the devil himself was on your tail and gainin'. Where were ya going in such a hurry?"

"Out for a ride," I said, still looking into my glass. "I needed some fresh air."

"If I hadn't seen it myself," he chuckled. "I never would have believed your old shovelhead could go like that."

I could see the concern in Lynn's eyes, but I had trouble paying much attention right then.

He continued babbling. "Lucky for you, our worthless sheriff was finally earning his pay trying to keep some idiot from robbing the 7-11."

I flagged Billy down again, ordering one for each of us. We sat in silence for a while, letting the J.D. cut through the road film. Finally, Lynn asked, "What's wrong, Bill? Where's Gina? You didn't let that little fox out on the streets alone, did you?"

"Gina's gone," I said. "She left this morning. She gave me some crap about being tired of me, my dog, my house, my worthless friends, and my 'piece a shit' motorcycle. Then she just left. I didn't even have a chance to talk about it." I looked down and rubbed my eyes. "Dammit, it's smoky in here. My eyes are burning."

Lynn sat there a minute, looking into his glass. "I'll be damned," he said thoughtfully. "I mean, I can understand her not liking you, and what can I say about your friends, if I'm any example, but calling that work of art, we spent God knows how many hours putting together 'a piece a shit' is going too far." Lynn gets a momentum going now and then. He had to have been a politician in a past life. I could see him mentally getting up on his imaginary soapbox. "Women think they can do anything they want just because they control half the money and all the sex in the world." He took a deep breath, grabbed both lapels on his jacket, and continued in his best Abraham Lincoln. "This situation calls for something above and beyond the norm, some kind of massive retaliation. Let me think about it a minute."

We both sat there a while reliving all the good and bad times we'd shared, all the women who had come and gone from our lives. I could see Lynn's mind turning over at warp speed. Finally, he broke out of his reverie and said, "I've got it. Tonight, I think some serious skirt chasin' is in order. There's nothin' like women to help you forget a woman. I heard a great band is playing at Bonge's, and Lippy said there were more sweet young things up there than any man in his right mind could want. He said they do a lot of Bob Seeger's old stuff. Let's ride."

The night air blew all of the memories of a blond-haired, green-eyed girl from my mind as we flew, wheel to wheel, up the twisting country roads to Bonge's. The moon was full, and the air was thick with the perfume of freshly plowed fields and spring flowers. Somehow my bike felt the newness of the season and the excitement of breaking away. She filled the night with her low rumble that had carried us through so many miles together. If anyone had seen Lynn and me on that ride, they would have understood what the brotherhood of bikers was all about. No two men were ever closer.

Lippy was right about Bonge's. Twelve Harleys were lined up in front, and "that old kind of rock 'n roll" was coming from inside.

Cars were parked up and down the street, so we backed our bikes in between a couple of very pretty Harleys. Lynn and I were admiring a chopper when a brunette came running out of the bar, threw her arms around Lynn, and gave him a kiss that would have suck-started any three of the Harleys. Suddenly her eyes snapped open, and she tried to hit him. "Who the Hell are you? You aren't Bob!"

"That's true," he said in his best Sam Elliott. "And you've only got three more chances to guess who I am." Then he gave her one of his easy smiles that let him get away with sayin' shit like that, took her arm, and went inside to get both of them a drink.

The night went by pretty fast after that. I met a redhead named Doris who "just *LOOOVVED* motorcycles" and spent a couple of hours in her van next to the bar. By the time two o'clock came around, Lynn and I were both pretty beat.

The first raindrops hit the gas tank as I kicked the motor to life. We went down the street slowly, getting the feel of the pavement. Already puddles were collecting in the roadway. The ride seemed a lot longer going back. The rain was coming down in sheets by then, driven by the wind going straight across the road. Sure we got wet, but it's not so bad after you feel the water trickle down the inside of your crotch. At least you can't get any wetter.

We were in a turn, going uphill, when the car that hit us came over the hill, lost it, and slid broadside into our lane. Lynn died instantly. I will die every day for the rest of my life. In a couple of years, I might even feel something below the neck.

It could be worse. Sometimes the nurse with the rose tattoo on her breast leaves the window open "by mistake", and I can hear a Harley or two go by before someone closes it again. The thing that hurts the most is I will never be able to say goodbye to Lynn.

"What do you mean?" the spirit beside my bed asked.

A spirit, an angel, or something very weird floated beside my bed. I looked over at Richard Cranium, the businessman in the bed next to me, but he was still heavily into watching his soap opera. Richard Cranium wasn't his name, of course, but Dick Head seemed too cruel.

"This must be some heavy shit they have me on." I chuckled, looking critically at the spirit—nice definition, as far as hallucinations go, but I'd seen better.

The spirit just looked back at me and smiled. "What do you mean?" it asked again.

I'm losing my mind. "Come on, you guys in the little white coats. The biker in room 14B has finally gone over the edge."

That got another screwed-up, benevolent smile from the spirit. "You said you wanted to say goodbye to Lynn. I can do that for you if you want."

OK, maybe I started goofing on it, I don't know. Maybe, I hoped it was a little bit true. Maybe, I was just completely over the edge and didn't give a damn anymore, but I started talking with the thing.

"How are you going to do that? Lynn's dead. They buried him last week."

I looked carefully at the spirit and wondered why this stuff always seemed to happen to me. I looked over at Richard again, but he was still staring at the tube with a bit of drool dripping off his chin. Soap operas will do that to you.

"How would you like to spend that last night with Lynn again? I mean, nothing would change in the end. Lynn would still die, and you would still end up here, paralyzed. But you would have a chance to say or do anything you wanted until that car hits you or whatever else happens when your time comes." He just stood there or whatever spirits do when they aren't doing whatever it is they do when they aren't right in front of you. I guess you may have noticed that this was seriously screwing with my mind.

As much as I didn't want to, I started to think about it. Another night! Riding one more time. The wind in my face. Feeling my bike rumble between my legs—a chance to tell Lynn all the things brothers never say until suddenly it's too late. I looked the spirit in the eye, or at least where its eyes would have been if it had eyes. "How do I know you're for real?" I asked. "I mean, nobody can go back in time. What's done is done."

He just smiled again, "Trust me. I can do it. All you have to do is say 'Yes'."

Maybe. Maybe he could do what he said. Maybe it was worth a shot. What the Hell. It wasn't like I'd had a lot of other offers. One more day whole had to be worth the rest of my life as a vegetable. "Done. I mean, 'Yes'. By the way, it's a little late to ask, but what's it cost, my soul or somethin'?"

"It doesn't cost anything. When I was here the last time, I built motorcycles in a shed behind my house in Milwaukee. My brothers, a friend, and I went into business together, but it was never the same as working together in that shed. Have a nice ride and twist the wick once for me." Then he was gone.

Richard had his mouth open, snoring quietly, the sun was going down outside, and I felt stupid, excited, and generally about like I would if my fly was open in the middle of a crowded shopping mall and no one noticed. My last thought as I slipped off to sleep was, "I wonder if I can save some of these meds to take home?"

....

I'll be damned. The old guy was as good as his word. Here I am, but I don't have a clue how I got here. The inside of the bar was still smoky. No one seemed to notice as I sat down and ordered some Jack Daniel's. "Straight up, Joe."

"Sure thing, Wild Bill." he smiled.

God, that tasted good. "Joe, hit me again." That one followed the first.

As I sipped my whiskey, I began to plan everything I would say and do on my last day before the crash.

"Lynn, I love ya." Nah, he'd just come back with some cute reply like, "Gee, big guy, want to go up to my place and get it on?" No, that didn't say it.

"Lynn, I just want to say what it means to me to have you as a ..." Geeze, where are the words? I sound like some damned school kid on his first date. The third Jack Daniel's arrived as Lynn walked through the door.

"Hey, Bill. Whatcha been up to?" he asked as he threw his leg over the stool.

I just stared into my glass, trying to grasp the right words. I must be some kind of wannabe. Here is my brother who is going to die tonight, and I can't even think of a way to tell him I love him and will miss him and ... *Dammit*!

Lynn looked at me carefully. "I saw you leaving town this morning like the devil himself was on your tail and gaining. Where were you going in such a hurry?"

"Out for a ride," I said, still looking into my glass. "I needed some fresh air."

Suddenly it became clear. This was Lynn's last night in this world, and I wasn't going to screw it up by being some goddammed bleeding heart. We both knew the end was waiting around the next corner. I couldn't think of a better goodbye than to share a night of riding and chasin' skirts with my closest brother in the world.

"Gina's gone," I said. "She left this morning. She gave me some crap about being tired of me, my dog, my house, my worthless friends, and my 'piece of shit' motorcycle. Then she just left. I didn't even have a chance to talk about it. Dammit, it's smoky in here. My eyes are burning."

We rode to Bonge's. Lynn got his kiss. I got Doris. We both had the best night of our lives again. After the bar closed and the rain started coming down, I looked over at Lynn and said, "Hey Lynn, this may sound weird, but I've always wanted to ride your bike. What say we trade for the ride home so's I can finally put that sexy little thing between my legs?"

"Sure, man. I always knew your bike was crying out for a real man."

On that same curve, Fate came slidin' over the hill.

A week later, Lynn lay in the hospital bed feeling sorry for himself, listening to the Harleys go by and wishing he could have said goodbye to me. The spirit beside his bed said, "What do you mean?"

The Wiz

"Bye, baby," Prissy shouted. "See ya in a little while."

She threw her leg over the back of the beat-up Harley with faded leather saddlebags and a scratched windshield. The scuzzy-looking biker reached back and squeezed her rear end as she settled onto the narrow seat. She gave a contented sigh and pressed her still trim body firmly into his. With a leering smile, he looked directly at Gayle, pulled Prissy's face to his, and noisily kissed her hard on the lips.

"Mom, please don't go. You promised you would spend some time with me." Gayle tried not to let her mother see the tears welling up in her twelve-year-old eyes.

The biker gave her a dirty look, then laughed and disappeared down the road with her mother wrapped around him like an octopus.

"Looks like you could use a new line to try on her," I said, leaning against the fence between our properties. "Not that it would make any difference. Your mother is a wild one."

"I hope she'll be OK," Gayle stammered. "Wiz, that guy scares me with the way he just takes anything he wants." She still stared down the dirt road where the dust of their departure was slowly clearing. "He's the worst of the lot she's hanging around with these days."

"Not all bikers are like that, Gayle." I smiled.

"I know, Wiz," she said, giving me a big hug. "You're great!"

"Why don't you help me plant these vegetables? Then, after lunch, *we* can go for a ride. I found this little country road last week. I think you'll love." I could see the worry in her eyes being replaced by happy expectations. I'd been worried, too, for the last several months. The guys her mother had been bringing home lately ... well ... Gayle was turning into a woman—going to be a *beautiful* woman in a couple of years. They saw it, too.

"God, help us all if anyone lays a finger on this little girl," I muttered. I'd lived next door to Prissy since Gayle was born, being resident babysitter, nurse, confessor, advisor, cry towel, and biker for both of them. Gayle's father never even knew Prissy was pregnant before someone killed him in a barroom fight over a game of nine-ball.

"She sure can pick 'em," I thought, shaking my head. "Probably better off *without* Gayle's father, for sure." He hadn't married either of the other two women he had gotten pregnant—didn't give a damn about *those* kids either. So why should I think he'd feel any different toward Gayle—definitely his loss.

By the time we finished planting potatoes, the road was callin' to me. I never could resist that lonely wench. I never even tried. But, yeah, OK, so I'm easy.

We got back from our ride about nightfall. All that fresh air had given me an appetite that gnawed at my belly like a grizzly bear. "Steak and potatoes in front of the tube sound OK?" I asked. She ate at my house more often than her own. "Maybe we can cook some popcorn later and find a B-Sci-Fi movie on NetFlix."

She looked up the road one last time, then said: "Sure, Wiz. Could we fix enough for Mom?"

"No problem," I said gently. If Prissy came home tonight, she would be roaring drunk and with her new beau. Food would be the last thing on her mind.

Gayle fell asleep about midnight after we had watched some fake rubber lobster-men get their claws blown off and cast back into the hot water pot of deep space, the Earth saved by the Japanese militia once again.

I stayed up, watching Gayle's face reflect the troubled dreams she saw on the other side. I had to admire her choice of a resting place. That sofa had been home-away-from-home for uncounted hordes of my friends needing a bed for the night. Of course, being within walking distance from the local watering hole didn't hurt its popularity, either.

The police came just before dawn. "Hey, Mike," I said, trying to wipe the sleep from my eyes. "You just getting off work?" Mike's the only cop I'd ever called my friend. We had ridden together since high school.

"We've got a problem with Prissy, Wiz."

"Where is she, man?" Shit, where would I get bail money on a Sunday?

"The morgue, Wiz." he said quietly, looking over at Gayle sleeping on the couch.

The impact of what he said slowly sank in. "What happened, Mike?"

"Near as we can figure, that guy she was with last night tried to get her to put out for his buddies. When she wouldn't do it, he beat her up, tied her to his bed, and they took turns. After a while, I guess they got tired of it, so he just blew her brains out—no witnesses and all that. You know how much fire she had in her. She was probably still spitting in his face as he pulled the trigger."

"The neighbors in his apartment building called 911 when they heard the gunshot. His buddies were carrying her out the back as we pulled up. We got everyone except the worm who started the whole mess. He won't get far. Every City, County, and State cop within a hundred miles is combing the countryside looking for him. We've got roadblocks everywhere."

"What's going to happen to Gayle?"

"As far as I'm concerned, she can stay with you for the time being. Hell, she pretty much lives here anyway. Family Services may not see it that way, though. If that's what you want, I'll do everything I can to help."

"What's going to happen to the men that did this to Mom?" Gayle asked, slowly getting up.

"Gayle, I'm so sorry," I said, holding out my arms. "I thought you were asleep."

She ran to me and held me tight as she began to cry great racking sobs.

Mike waited until the worst of it had passed, then he said, "Gayle, I promise you they will go to jail for a long time. I know that won't bring back your mom, but it's the best we can do. The courts don't allow the kind of punishment these monsters deserve."

"I need both of you to help us find him," he continued. "Gayle, I understand a lot of his stuff is in your house. We suspect he will try to return for it before leaving the area. So we want to put an officer in Wiz's house to watch yours. Is that all right, Wiz?"

"Of course, man," I said with a grim smile. "But I would *really* like to be the one that finds him."

"Wiz, just let *us* do our job! Don't try to confront this guy. He's already killed once, and he knows we know it. If you get in his way, he'll run over you like a dog in the road and laugh."

"OK," I said without looking at him. I could tell he didn't believe me, but he also knew he couldn't do anything about it.

"Wiz, I mean it! Leave this guy *alone*. You're all Gayle has right now, and she needs you alive."

He introduced his partner, who would stake out Gayle's house in the unmarked car out front, then he left. I walked slowly into the kitchen to make some coffee and came face-to-face with slime-ball himself.

"Hi, asshole. Looking for me?"

He had a very efficient-looking 9 MM automatic in his hand pointed in my general direction. "Just stopped by to pick up a few things before I'm off. That was good advice your friend gave you. Are you going to listen to it?"

"Leave the girl alone, and you can have anything you want," I said quietly. "Here's the keys to my truck. I won't report it missing for four hours."

"I always knew I could count on you, Wiz," he sneered. "Nice and *yellow,* just like your name says." He took the keys and motioned me into the corner with his pistol. He took my last beer from the refrigerator. "Mind?" he asked.

"No. Take the wine, too."

"Think I'll get drunk and wreck? Not on this soda pop." He reached back into the refrigerator and retrieved the bottle.

"Out back! Now!" He motioned me toward the door.

"Turn off the alarm, and start the truck." He kept the 9 MM trained on my chest. "Now is *not* the time for heroics, Wiz."

When the truck was running, I got out, and he slid over to the driver's seat. "See ya around, Wiz." he smirked, "Cheat on the four hours, and I'll be back for fun and games with the little girl that'll make her mother's playtime look like Sesame Street." Then he was gone.

It didn't take four hours for the cops to find him. He had run off a straight road into a cornfield about twenty miles away. No, he wasn't hurt. At least not by the wreck. My truck was hardly damaged at all. Slime-ball was sitting in the cab listening to the radio and making little humming noises, kind of like a lawnmower, going fast, then slow, over and over, the empty wine bottle clasped in his arms.

You see, I had a friend who used to make a lot of LSD. One day he went too far and vowed never to touch the stuff again. He gave me his bottle full of acid-laced wine to keep until he dried out enough to get rid of it. Must have been at least two hundred good Dead Head hits in that bottle. I expect slime-ball will have the rest of his life to remember those colors while he enjoys the companionship of his cellmate in the state prison.

They Don't Have Christmas in Vietnam

I drove a truck. I may have worn jungle fatigues, carried an M-16, and put a steel helmet on my head, but the reality was: I drove a truck. Since being assigned to the 359th Transportation Company in Quy Nhon, South Vietnam, the 5,000-gallon tanker full of fuel had been my companion for four months. We'd driven north, south, and west from Quy Nhon, delivering diesel, aviation gas, and motor fuel to whichever American base or LZ needed it.

My tour was almost over. Everyone knew the war was winding down. We weren't getting hit much. A lot of guys weren't wearing their flack vests and helmets while they drove those damned hot, noisy trucks. In December of 1970, I hoped the army would show a bit of olive-drab compassion and send me home a few days early—"Christmas at home" apparently as great a fiction as a cool day in Vietnam.

I would pick up a load from the fuel storage facility in Quy Nhon, near the coast in the center of South Vietnam. From there, I would pull the fuel into the central highlands to An Khe or Pleiku or up or down the coast to off-load it at one landing zone or another. The following day I'd drive back to Quy Nhon and do it all over again. There aren't any days off in a combat zone. We worked sixteen to twenty hours a day, slept when we could, and toughed it out. On a good day, I got to sleep in my bunk at the company barracks outside of Quy Nhon. The mess sergeant always had food ready for people who came in late. A hot shower, clean clothes, a belly full of food that didn't come from a C-ration box—these were the things that were the Holy Grail of my life.

I kept hoping for my orders to come down, so I could begin to clear the base and go home. On December 20th, the company clerk told me I wasn't leaving until my scheduled rotation date in January. That meant I was here through Christmas and New Year.

December 23rd, I unloaded my jet fuel at an Air Force base north of Quy Nhon, then carried a load of diesel to the Special Forces at Tuy Hoa, farther to the south. After that, I pulled jet fuel to the Fourth Infantry Division at An Khe and spent the night there, listening to helicopters flying in and out. The next morning, I drove back to Quy Nhon and topped off my tanker with JP4, the jet fuel the choppers used. I was hoping for a short run up or down the coast. That would mean I could have the Christmas present of a night in the lap of luxury of my bunk.

As I pulled my rig into the motor pool, my motor sergeant ran up to me with a big smile. That was never a good thing. "You're loaded with JP4! Cool! A convoy to Pleiku is leaving from **Charang** Valley in twenty minutes. This is a special delivery. The 101st is almost out of fuel for their choppers. You can make it tonight."

"That means I'll be in Pleiku on Christmas, Sarge!"

"They don't have Christmas in Vietnam, soldier. Didn't you know that?" He laughed and turned away, calling over his shoulder, "See you when you get back."

The drive to Pleiku took at least twelve hours. It was already past noon. This day would be a long one.

December in Vietnam has a special kind of hot and dry weather which creates a special kind of dust. The first truck in the convoy puts the dust up into the air. The rest of us get to enjoy the dust and make it better. The poor bastard at the end doesn't have a chance. This dust is so fine and loose that even raindrops kick up clouds of it when a storm passes. Then the dust gets wet and turns into the slipperiest, slimiest, most evil grease you can ever imagine trying to drive over. You can't even look at a wet road in Vietnam without your gaze sliding off to the side.

That dust finds its way into everything. You'd think, "I have pants on. It can't possibly get inside my pants." You'd be wrong. No part of your body is sacred or immune to the dust of Vietnam. After four days on the road without a shower or clean clothes, you could peel the collected dust off your body like dried-on paint.

It was after midnight by the time we got to Pleiku. "Merry Christmas!" I told the gate sentry. He just laughed and waved me through.

I off-loaded my fuel and parked my truck in the RON (Remain Over Night) area. I got my shaving kit, an almost clean towel, and some nearly clean clothes and walked to the shower area the drivers used.

"Don't waste your time," a driver said in disgust, returning from the showers with his clean clothes still over his arm. "There's no water."

"You mean no *hot* water?" I asked hopefully.

"I mean no water. Hot, cold, warm, smelly, clean. Not in the showers, sinks, or toilets. Nothing. The goddamned floor's even dry."

No water. No shower. Crap.

I scratched the four-day stubble on my cheek. OK, it wasn't much stubble. I was only twenty-two and blonde, but it was there, and I didn't want it to be. And I had the problem of my sleeping bag—crawling into my sleeping bag without at least a washcloth bath wasn't going to happen. I was a walking, reeking dirtball.

"Screw this," I muttered, tucking my shaving kit, clothes, and towel under my arm. I set out with a new resolve to take a shower. Somewhere on this base, some water was hiding, and I would find it. I walked and walked. I passed barracks with guys smoking on the steps but no water. I found a garden hose next to the NCO club, but only a hiss came out when I turned the nozzle.

By 2 A.M., I had given **up, realizing I would spend the rest of Christmas Eve enjoying my smelly armpits inside my sleeping bag.** I had one canteen of water in my truck. It would have to do. So, feeling about as low as whale-shit, I began the long walk back to the RON area. Then, as I passed the Officer's Club, something completely unexpected happened. Behind the Officer's Club was an oasis, an apparition, the answer to my wildest dreams—beckoning to me like a smiling young woman, full of seduction and delight—the Officer's Club had a swimming pool!

I paused, leaning on the four-foot chain-link fence, trying to look casual, while I checked in all directions—no one in sight.

In a flash, I was over the fence and pulling my clothes off. I eased into the water, making as little noise as possible. As strange as it sounds, I felt like I was sliding into a twenty-thousand-gallon bathtub—the water was at least 90 degrees. I pulled out my soap and washed my smelly body from head to toe. I dug out all the dirt from under my fingernails. I scrubbed all those private places that were very happy to be clean again. I got my shampoo and washed my hair—twice. **Finally,** I fished my razor and shaving cream from my kit and shaved. "Lots of water here," I laughed, watching the little islands of shaving foam drift away to the deep end.

I'm sure the following day, some PFC was cussing me for the mess I made while he vacuumed the dirt from the bottom of the pool. But that night, as I floated on my back in that warm water, looking up at the stars on Christmas morning in Pleiku, all I could think of were the words to Louis Armstrong's song—what a wonderful world!

When Is a Kiss Not a Kiss

I taught my first data processing officer course at the Army Institute of Administration at Fort Harrison, Indiana, after being a second lieutenant for all six months. My class of 29 officers varied in rank from second lieutenant up to lieutenant colonel. We were a few days into their introduction to the COBOL computer programming language. Many of the young officers already had computer programming while in college. Those young men and women charged ahead with energy and easy success. The older officers struggled.

The army had decided all of its officers, especially combat officers, had to have a second, noncombat, specialty. The data processing officer course was the plum that everyone tried to get. The problem was those senior officers were no longer detail-oriented. They had grown very used to making decisions and then delegating the details to their staff. The detail-oriented parts of their brains had gotten a little rusty from un-use, and computer programming is very detail-oriented.

Those captains, majors, and the lieutenant colonel had trouble accepting that the lieutenants could excel at something while they, as older officers, could not. So they tried harder.

They were making all of the mistakes that new programmers make. Their solutions were too complicated. They would box themselves into a blind alley with their program logic and couldn't figure out how to fix it. They should have corrected their design and then re-coded. What they did was add to what they had already written, making it more and more complicated. A bad design can never become a good program.

Finally, in frustration, I tried to get their attention by using an acronym I had learned in OBC (Officer Basic Course) three months earlier. The army has acronyms for everything, and if you use an acronym, your credibility goes up by at least 50%. People have made a career in the army by creating and using acronyms.

"Class," I announced to them proudly. "Remember the K.I.S.S. principle."

They all paused from their efforts and looked up at me. I could see in their eyes they were ready for the new second lieutenant to say something dumb. K.I.S.S. meant, Keep It Simple Stupid.

I began my explanation of the phrase. "Keep it simple …" and I stopped as I looked into the eyes of the lieutenant colonel. I knew if I finished the phrase, I would be in deep do-do. There was no way a second lieutenant could get away with calling a collection of captains, majors, and a lieutenant colonel stupid.

The lieutenant colonel looked at me with amusement, clearly wondering how I would salvage my lesson. My pause grew longer and longer, and my face got redder and redder. The whole class became silent. Everyone in the room knew how the acronym ended and knew just as clearly that I had put myself into a spot.

Finally, a captain in the front row raised his hand and finished it for me. "Keep it simple, *sir*."

He saved my butt.

I used that acronym in every class I taught after that, always drawing out the suspense of the last word before saying "sir" instead of "stupid." It got a laugh every time. After those officers graduated and continued their military careers as data processing officers, I hoped they remembered getting KISSed in COBOL class and kept their solutions simple.

Fredrick Hudgin

Author's Notes

If you liked this book, please do a review of it on
GoodReads.com
or Amazon.com, if you bought it from them.
It's reviews that sell books and help me fund my
next novel.
Thanks - Fred

A Rainy Night
> Fiction. Inspired by reading H. R. Munroe's (AKA Saki) *The Open Window*. This is my wife's favorite of my short stories. In another life, I think she was the little girl.

The Captain's Gold
> Fiction. What fun to write! My first real sex scene.

Ashes on the Ocean
> Fiction. Inspired by an office conversation. Published at The Last Girl's Club.

The Job
> What do you do when your son still lives at home and the college where he's been a freshman for seven years kicks him out?

Being Dad
> Fiction. My son did not die in Afghanistan. This story is a composite of what two of my friends felt when their sons died, and what I imagine I would have felt if one of my sons had joined theirs.

Get Them OFF!
> Non-Fiction. I still chuckle about that old woman driving by. Mom tried to figure out who it was so she could explain. She never did find out.

Gina

Fiction. This is the first chapter of my novel *Ghost Ride*. The Special Forces have the toughest job in the Army. My hat is off to them. I wrote this as a short story and sent it to my friends. They said "You have GOT to write the rest of the book." So I did.

Paradise

Fiction. This is the first chapter of my novel *Green Grass*. I wrote this also as a short story and sent it to my friends. They said the same thing they did for Gina. So wrote this also.

Longest Ride

Fiction. What do you do when your wife of twenty years calls you up after a six-month separation and wants to restart the only relationship in your life that has ever meant anything? You go to her. But the Gods were playing that day, and you die before you reach her. Instead of the fire pits or wings and halos you expected, you are put on an endless motorcycle ride. You can go fast or slow, but you can't stop. Your only companions are the demons who ride next to you, until the day that you figure out a way to ride with Mr. Fire and Brimstone himself.

Jack the Cat

Fiction. My kids and I were talking about how important pets were to disabled people's recovery. My daughter helps vets with PTSD overcome their demons with horses and horse training. The idea for this story came out of one of those meetings.

A Call in the Middle of the Night

Non-fiction. This was the only time in all my blood donations that I actually witnessed the use of my blood in saving someone's life.

Nice Day for a Ride

Fiction. I also created a sci-fi version of this called A Nice Day for a Wormhole Ride. This was published in

Biker Magazine, August 2011, two issues before they went out of business.

Ha

Non-fiction. This was a tough one to write. When I came home from Vietnam, I put all the unhappy memories in a box at the back of my mind and sealed it with mental tape, never to be opened again. But this story has escaped many times. I can still see Ha being driven away in that jeep, like it was yesterday. You think life in a war zone is tough on the fighters, but most people don't realize how tough it is on the non-fighters. I've replayed the encounter over and over a thousand time and never have figured out what I could have done to change the outcome. Now I'm watching the same stuff happen in Ukraine. Bodies of children lined up on the sidewalk with their parents. It breaks my heart. Childhood should be a happy time, not one filled with fear, hiding, bombs, and bullets. Maybe that's why I finally decided to put this down on paper. It's been fifty-one years since I came home from that damned war, and I suppose I'm still healing.

Who Was Eve Really

Fiction. I love alternate history. I wrote this while I was trying to figure out how all of humanity could be descended from a single human female, Eve. I couldn't understand why we didn't look like that scene in *Deliverance*. So I asked myself, what if the Adam and Eve story in the *Bible* was a metaphor instead of being literal? With this story, Eve's DNA was simply used to identify who was going to be raised up, not as a contributor to the actual genetic process. That way the genetic diversity of the participants would remain intact and humanity would have a starting gene-pool of tens of thousands instead of just two.

Then I decided this was alternate history and why not make it a little more fun. What if someone else raised up another species at the same time; claim jumpers like the old west! And have the claim jumpers be Mer people! This became the opening chapter of *The Beginning of the End*, Book One in the *End of Children* series.

The Chair
Non-Fiction. That chair still sits next to my dining room table until someday it will go to one of my kids.

Coming Home
Non-Fiction. My trip home from the war. The only thing stranger than fiction is truth. I actually thought about being a cop after I came home into a full-blown recession.

The Mission
Fiction. But anyone who had gone to Daytona during Bike Week will have their own share of stories to tell.

The Second Chance
Fiction. Pure whimsy—a fantasy infinite loop.

The Wiz
Fiction. My first attempt at adventure fiction.

They Don't Have Christmas in Vietnam
Non-Fiction. I wonder if that swimming pool is still there. This was published in *That Holiday Feeling*—a collection of Christmas stories.

When Is a Kiss Not a Kiss
Non-Fiction. After I finished my degree in computer science at Rutgers University, I was commissioned a second lieutenant in the Army because I also took ROTC as an undergraduate. I taught computer programming at Fort Harrison, IN, for a year and a half before I left the Army and began working for real

Fredrick Hudgin

as a computer programmer. This was published in *Not Your Mother's Book on Working for a Living.*

Fredrick Hudgin

I have been writing poetry and short stories since I took a Creative Writing class at Purdue University in 1967. Unfortunately, that was the only class I passed, and I spent the next three years in the Army, including a tour in Vietnam. After leaving the Army, I earned a BS in Computer Science from Rutgers and struck off on a career as a professional computer programmer and amateur poet.

I find that my years of writing poetry have affected how I write prose. My wife keeps telling me to put more narrative into the story. My poetry side keeps trying to pare it down to the emotional bare bones. What I create is always a compromise between the two.

Short stories and poems of mine have been published in Biker Magazine, two compilations by Poetry.Com, The Salal Review, The Scribbler, That Holiday Feeling—a collection of Christmas short stories, The Preservation Foundation, The Last Girls Club, and Not Your Mother's Book on Working for a Living.

My home is in Ariel, Washington, with my wife, two horses, two dogs, and four cats. I volunteer at my local fire department as an EMT/Firefighter.

All my books and short stories are for sale on Amazon in hardcopy or e-book form. Do a search for "Fredrick Hudgin".

Books Books by
Fredrick Hudgin
All are available at Amazon.com

Sulphur Springs – Historical Fiction — Set in Lewis County, Washington

A novel about two women who settle in the Northwest. Washington State didn't want the ex-slaves to come there from the South. This book showcases the racism present in Washington State in 1895. Black people couldn't vote or own property. A very active chapter of the Ku Klux Klan was in Chehalis. The land the Cowlitz tribes had lived on for thousands of years was taken from them without compensation and given to the white settlers.

Duha (pronounced DooHa) is the daughter of a slave midwife. She and her mother are determined to escape the racism in Independence, Missouri, by migrating to Washington State in 1895. But her mother dies in Sheridan, Wyoming, leaving Duha with no money, job, or future beyond working in the brothels. She meets Georgia Prentice, a nurse in the hospital where her mother dies. Georgia takes her in, and together, they begin a life that spans sixty years and three generations.

They settle in the quiet, idyllic settlement of Sulphur Springs, Washington, nestled between three volcanoes—Mt Rainier, Mt Adams, and Mt St Helens. The beautiful fir-covered hills and crystal-clear rivers belie the evil growing there that threatens to swallow Duha's and Georgia's families. Three generations must join together as a psychotic rapist/murderer threatens to destroy everything they have worked and suffered to create.

Ghost Ride – Fantasy/Action-Thriller — Loose sequel to Sulphur Springs. David is the great-grandson of Duha. Rhiannon is the great-granddaughter of Georgia.

A novel about how ghosts share our lives and interact with us daily, usually without us having the slightest clue we are talking to a ghost.

David is a Green Beret medic. At least he was for thirty years until he retired and returned to his parents' home without a clue about what to do with the rest of his life.

While trying to figure out how to recover from the violence he'd faced in Afghanistan and Iraq, he meets a woman who shows him the way and then disappears.

As David rebuilds his parents' home and attempts to start an emergency care clinic in his rural town, he meets the woman's granddaughter. Together they figure out how to bring down the meth lab that has poisoned their rural town, overcome state licensing regulations preventing the clinic from opening, help their friend attempt to beat his cancer, and discover David's roots buried in an Indian sweat lodge.

Ghosts abound in this story of love, betrayal, supernatural guides, and unfaithful parents. The good guys aren't entirely good. The bad guys aren't entirely bad. Nothing is what it seems at first glance in Chambersville as the book leads the reader on a merry Ghost Ride.

School of the Gods – Fantasy

A novel about the balance between good and evil.

The idea for **The School of the Gods** began with a series of what-ifs. What if we did have multiple lives? What if God made mistakes and learned from them? What if our spiritual goal was to become a god, and it was his job to foster us while we grew? What if we ultimately became the god of our universe, responsible for fostering our own crop of spirits to godhead? If all that were true, there would have to be a school. I mean, that's what schools do—give us the training to start a new career.

The School of the Gods is not a book about God, religious dogma, or organized religion. Instead, it's a story about Jeremiah—ex-Marine, bar fly, and womanizer. Jeremiah's life of excess leads to an untimely end. There is nothing unusual about his death other than he is the 137,438,953,472nd person to die since the beginning of humanity. That coincidence allows Jeremiah to bypass Judgement and get a free pass into Heaven. It also begins the story.

Jeremiah's entry into the hereafter leads him to become the confidant of our universe's god. As Jeremiah begins his path toward godhead, he discovers the answer to many questions about God that have confounded humanity from the beginning of time: why transsexuals exist, the real reason for the ten commandments, why the Great Flood of Noah actually happened, and where the other species that couldn't fit on the boat were kept. Along the way,

God, Jeremiah, and three other god-hopefuls throw the forces of evil out of God's Home, create a beer drinker's guide to the universes, and become all-powerful gods of their own universes.

Four Winds – A collection of Poetry

A collection of poetry in two parts: Poems about love, tears, hope, and fears. Poems that are *not* about love, tears, hope, and fears. Some rhyme—some don't. Some are silly—some are serious. They encompass the beginning of my written career through my current efforts. They lay the groundwork for the prose that I have created. If you can't write about things you experience, you probably need to do something else. And like anything else, you get better with practice. I was tempted to put them into chronological order, but after so many years of polishing and correcting, who knows what the actual date should be? Or I could have put them in order of my most favorite to my less favorite. But your order would be different because everyone resonates with poems differently. So, I decided to make them alphabetical.

Green Grass – Fantasy/Adventure

This is my first young-reader (12-year-olds and higher) book. My grandkids kept asking me for one of my books. Those books were all full of adult words, thoughts, and actions—clearly not appropriate for young readers. So, I wrote this one.

I'm sure you've heard the cliché about the grass always being greener. Sometimes it's true—

sometimes it's not. It's usually a little more complicated than that.

There are no adult words beyond what I hear tweens use every day. And no sex beyond holding hands, giving hugs, and kissing. While the book contains some violence and death, it is not graphic, and I feel it is presented in a way that most young readers would understand without getting disturbed.

However, being a young reader book doesn't mean that the plots and subplots are not interesting. Susannah and her friends are dropped into the middle of a civil war. There are good people and bad people on both sides of the portal. Deciding who is who becomes a pretty important question to figure out. After the Earthlings get cloned, things really get complicated. Imagine saying "Hi!" to yourself!

So, pull up a chair and enter a world of Magic with dragons, mages, and swords. It is called Gleepth. You can only get there once a year and only for a few minutes. But no one told Susannah when she stepped into the portal and into a life beyond anything she had ever dreamed of. And there was no way back beyond waiting a year for the next window.

The End of Children Trilogy – Science Fiction

The End of Children has SEX. It has ALIENS WHO WANT TO CRUSH US and ALIENS WHO WANT TO HELP. It has VIRUSES. It has PRESIDENTIAL CORRUPTION. It has GALACTIC WARS. It has KIDNAPPED BABIES. It has INTELLIGENT PORPOISES, and they don't hitchhike!

Some kids find out how to open a wormhole, the government weaponizes it, the wormhole detectors on the moon announce the discovery to the rest of the galaxy, and after the aliens make humanity sterile for being too warlike and put us in an airtight quarantine, we have World War III. It takes three hours to decimate almost all the governments and military of the world – thank god for Canada! The world's male leaders have failed us, and the galaxy won't talk to us about a second chance.

But it all ends happily. A brave young woman finally convinces the galaxy we have something to contribute by performing *Romeo and Juliette* by herself in a space capsule with two weeks of food and no way to return to Earth. Our galaxy gets attacked by another galaxy. We save the emperor of our galaxy, show his generals how to fight after ten thousand years of peace, and kick the other galaxy's ass. The emperor offers us another world. We turn over Earth to the porpoises, emigrate to the new world (named Atlantis), and get admitted to the Ur with the woman as our representative.

OK. I left out a little. It's a big story, told in three volumes, each with over 100,000 words.

This is the story of how it all unfolds.

Book 1 – The Beginning of the End

Book 2 – The Three-Hour War

Book 3 – The Emissary

Made in United States
Troutdale, OR
01/24/2025